LAUGH YOUR HEAD OFF AGAIN AND AGAIN!

Pan Macmillan acknowledges the Traditional Custodians of country throughout Australia and their connections to lands, waters and communities. We pay our respect to Elders past and present and extend that respect to all Aboriginal and Torres Strait Islander peoples today. We honour more than sixty thousand years of storytelling, art and culture.

First published 2017 in Macmillan by Pan Macmillan Australia Pty Ltd
This Pan edition published 2022 by Pan Macmillan Australia Pty Ltd
1 Market Street, Sydney, New South Wales, Australia, 2000

Cataloguing-in-Publication entry is available from the National Library of Australia
http://catalogue.nla.gov.au

Typeset in 11.5/17pt Charter by i2i Design
Printed by IVE Group

The paper in this book is FSC® certified.
FSC® promotes environmentally responsible, socially beneficial and economically viable management of the world's forests.

LAUGH YOUR HEAD OFF AGAIN AND . . .

illustrations
by
Andrea
Innocent

PAN
Pan Macmillan Australia

AGAIN!

CONTENTS

IN THE SHOWER WITH ANDY

by

Andy Griffiths

I'm in the shower. Singing. And not just because the echo makes my voice sound so cool either. I'm singing because I'm so happy.

Ever since I've been old enough to have showers I've been trying to find a way to fill a shower cubicle up with water. If I put a face-washer over the plughole I can get the water as far up as my ankles, but it always ends up leaking out through the gaps in the door.

But I think I've finally found the answer—Dad's silicone gun.

I've plugged up the plughole.

I've sealed up the shower-screen doors.

I've even filled in all the cracks in the tiles.

The cubicle is completely watertight and the water is already up to my knees.

And the best thing is that I've got all night to enjoy it.

Mum and Dad have got Mr and Mrs Bainbridge over for dinner. They'll be too busy listening to Mr Bainbridge talking about himself to have time to worry about what I'm doing.

I hear banging on the door.

'Have you almost finished, Andy?'

It's Jen!

'No,' I say. 'I think I'm going to be in here a while yet.'

'Can you hurry up?' yells Jen.

'But you already had your shower this morning,' I yell.

'I'm going out,' she says. 'I need the bathroom!'

'Okay. I'll be out in a minute,' I call. I always say that. It's the truth. Sort of. I will be out in a minute—I'm just not saying which minute it will be.

The cubicle is filling with thick white steam. Just the way I like it. Dad's always telling us how important it is to turn the fan on when we're having a shower, but I can't see the point. A shower without steam doesn't make sense. You might as well go and stand outside in the rain.

My rubber duck bumps against my legs. I pick it up.

'This is it,' I say. 'Just you and me . . . going where no boy—or rubber duck—has ever gone before.'

It has its bill raised in a sort of a smile. It must be as excited as I am. Let's face it, there can't be that much excitement in the life of a rubber duck. Except that you'd get to see everybody without their clothes on.

Jen bangs on the door again.

'Andy! Pleeeeease!'

'Okay,' I call. 'I'll be out in a minute.'

'You said that a minute ago.'

'I'm washing my hair.'

'But you've been in there for at least half an hour. You don't have *that* much hair.'

'I'm using a new sort of shampoo—I have to do it strand by strand.'

'Andy!'

The water is almost up to my belly-button.

There's only one thing missing. Bubbles!

I pick up the bubblebath and measure out a capful. I tip it into the water. A few bubbles, but not enough. I add another cap. And another. And another. One more for good measure. Another for good luck.

I keep adding bubblebath until the bottle is empty. The bubbles rise over my head. Cool. It's like I'm being eaten by this enormous white fungus. Well, not that being eaten by an enormous white fungus would be cool—it would probably be quite uncool, actually—but you know what I mean.

Jen is yelling.

'Andy, if you don't get out right this minute, you're going to be sorry.'

Jen is persistent, I'll give her that. But I'll fix her. I'll use my old 'what did you say?' routine.

'Pardon?' I yell. 'What did you say?'

'I said you're going to be sorry!'

'What? I can't hear you!'

'I said get out of the shower!'

'Pardon?'

No reply. I win.

Aaaagghhh!

The water's gone hot! Boiling hot!

Jen must have flushed the toilet. That's bad news.

I lose.

I jump back against the shower wall.

Hot water splatters onto my face. My chest. My arms.

I grab the cold tap and turn it on full.

The hot water disappears. Now it's freezing.

I'm going to have to turn both taps off and start all over again. I hate that. Being a pioneer is not easy.

I turn the hot tap off. But the cold won't budge.

I grab the tap with both hands. I try to twist it clockwise but it's stuck. Not even my super-strength can move it.

The silicone gun is hanging off the shower pipe. I pick it up and start bashing the tap with it. That should loosen it.

But the handgrip shatters.

The pieces disappear into the soapy water. I'm staring at a thin metal rod coming out of the wall. And the water is still flowing full blast.

I kneel down and clamp my teeth over the tap rod.

No good. The tap feels like it's rusted into place. My teeth will crack before it moves.

There's no steam left. The bubbles have been flattened. The freezing water is almost up to my chest. Maybe this wasn't such a great idea.

Time to bail out.

I take a deep breath and dive to the bottom of the shower. I'm trying to find the plughole. I've got to get the silicone out before the shower fills up completely.

But I can't do it. I did the job too well. There's nothing but a hard rubbery slab of silicone where the plug used to be. I can't poke through it. I can't get a fingernail underneath to lift it up. It's times like this I wish I didn't bite my nails. But then it's times like this that cause me to bite my nails in the first place.

I stand up, gasping for air. The water is up to my neck. I grab hold of the doorhandle and try to wrench it open but I laid the silicone even thicker on the doors than the plughole. If you ever want anything sealed tight I can recommend Dad's silicone gun. This stuff stays stuck forever.

I'm going to have to break the door down.

I'll use the gun. It made short work of the tap so the door shouldn't be a problem.

I bash the glass with the gun handle. It bounces off. I bash it again, harder this time. The gun snaps in two. Just my luck. Reinforced shower screen glass. Unbreakable.

I'm shivering. And not just from the cold. I'm scared.

I start bashing the door with the duck.

'HELP! I'M DROWNING! HELP!'

'I'm not surprised!' Jen yells back. 'You've been in there long enough.'

'Jen, I'm not kidding. Help me!'

'What did you say?' she says. 'I can't hear you.'

'Be serious,' I yell. 'I've siliconed myself in here.'

'What?'

She wins again.

I'm treading water. My head is very close to the top of the shower.

The only way I can save myself is to get rid of the water.

I'm going to have to drink it.

Dirty soapy shower water.

I'd rather die.

The water nudges the tip of my nose.

Actually, on second thoughts I'd rather drink the water.

I start swallowing.

It's working. I just have to drink as fast as the shower is filling up. And if I can drink even faster then I might get out of here alive yet. Actually the water doesn't taste that bad—it's only been three days since my last shower.

I keep swallowing.

And swallowing. And swallowing. And swallowing.

Uh-oh.

I can't believe this.

I need to go to the toilet.

But I can't.

I'll drink dirty shower water but I won't drink that.

I've got to hold on.

But I can't do that, either.

I'm busting.

▲ ▲ ▲

My head is bumping against the roof of the shower.

It's getting harder to breathe.

There's more banging on the door but it sounds like it's coming from a long way away.

'I'm going to tell Dad,' says Jen in a distant voice. 'Is that what you want? Is it?'

'Yes, Jen,' I call. 'Yes! Please hurry!'

Everything becomes quiet.

My life is flashing before my eyes.

I see myself blowing a high-pitched whistle while Mum is trying to talk on the telephone. I see myself letting down the tyres on Dad's car. I see myself hiding a rubber snake in Jen's bed. Is that all I did with my life? Annoy people? Surely I did something useful . . . something good?

Nope. I can't think of anything. Except for solving the problem of how to fill a shower cubicle with water.

I may be going to die, but at least it will be a hero's death. Future generations of Australian children will thank me as they float around in their sealed-up shower cubicles.

Ouch!

Something is pressing into the top of my head.

I look up.

The fan! I forgot all about it.

It's not very big, but it's better than nothing. If I can get the grille off then I can escape through the hole and up into the roof.

I work my fingers under the edge of the grille and pull on it. It comes off easily.

I reach into the casing and grab hold of the fan. I rock it back and forth. There is a little bit of give in it. I start giving it all I've got.

Finally the bolts holding it give way. I push my arms and head into the hole, kicking like mad to get the thrust I need to make it all the way up.

The opening is smaller than I thought. I expel every last bit of air in my lungs to make myself thin enough to fit through the hole. Not that there was much air left in them, but it seems to help.

At last! I'm through!

I'm lying on a yellow insulation batt in the roof of

our house. The glass fibres are prickly on my skin, but I'm not complaining. It's a lot better than where I was. I look back into the hole. It's like one of those fishing holes that Eskimos cut in the ice. But there's no fish. Just my rubber duck. I reach down and pick it out. We're in this together. I can't just leave it.

After I get my breath back I look around.

I know there's a manhole in the top of the kitchen. All I have to do is locate it, climb down into the kitchen and nick down the hallway into my room. Then I can put my pyjamas on and go to bed early. It will save a lot of boring explanation—and, if I'm really lucky, Jen will get the blame.

I have to move fast. I start crawling towards the kitchen. I'm carrying the duck in one hand and using my other hand to feel my way along the roof beam.

Suddenly I feel a sharp pain in my thumb. I jerk my hand back and almost lose my balance. I fling the duck away so I can grab the beam with my other hand.

I look at my thumb. A huge splinter is sticking out of it. I pull it out with my teeth. Ouch!

I shake my hand a few times and look around for my duck. It has landed in the middle of a large unsupported section of insulation batts. I'm tempted to leave it there. But that wouldn't be right. It's been with me all the way. I can't abandon it now.

I reach towards it but it's too far away. I'm going to have to crawl out there. I know you're not supposed to climb on the unsupported parts of the roof, but I think it will be okay. I'm not that heavy. And it's not as if I have any clothes on to weigh me down.

I climb carefully onto the batts and start moving slowly to the centre. One more metre and I'm there.

I pick up my duck and bring it up to my face. 'Just you and me,' I say.

The duck creaks. That's weird. I didn't know rubber ducks could talk.

Uh-oh. The creaking is not coming from the duck. It's coming from underneath me. The ceiling is giving way.

I try to grab the roof beam but I can't reach it.

The ceiling caves in.

Next thing I know I'm lying, legs spread, in the middle of the dinner table—my fall broken by an insulation batt.

As the dust from the ceiling plaster settles, I see Mr and Mrs Bainbridge and Mum and Dad staring down at me.

Jen is standing next to Dad, her bath towel draped over her shoulder. Her back is turned towards me and she's so busy complaining to Dad that she doesn't seem to notice what has happened.

'. . . I've asked him a million times but he just won't get out . . . ' she's saying.

'Oh, dear,' says Mum.

'Oh, my,' says Mrs Bainbridge.

For once in his life Mr Bainbridge is speechless.

'Oh, no,' says Dad, shaking his head at me. 'No, no, no!'

'Oh yes,' says Jen. 'And I'll tell you what else . . . '

Dad nods in my direction.

Jen stops, turns around and stares.

I cover myself with the rubber duck, swing my legs over the edge of the table and stand up.

'I beg your pardon,' I say. 'I was looking for the kitchen.'

Nobody says anything. They are all just staring at me, their faces and clothes white from the plaster dust.

I head towards the door as fast as I can.

As I'm about to exit I turn towards Jen. She is still standing there, eyes wide.

'Well, what are you waiting for?' I say. 'Shower's free!'

MR WOLF PIE

by

R. A. Spratt

Peter, Luke and Lucy were three lovely children, and their parents were good hardworking people. But there comes a point in every school holidays when even the nicest child will start to drive even the kindest parent mad. No matter how much a parent loves their child there is a limit to how many snacks they can fix before they want to tear their hair out and scream, 'For goodness sake, can I just have one moment of peace without someone asking me to fetch a SAO cracker?' You have probably heard your own parents say something similar.

It is at this point that any sensible parent takes action, and arranges for their sweet angels to spend a few days with their grandmother.

Peter, Lucy and Luke did not mind this at all. They loved being sent to Granny's house. Granny had no limits on the consumption of chocolate, no qualms about letting them use her power tools and she absolutely insisted that they spend hours watching reality TV with her because she thoroughly enjoyed watching regular people humiliate themselves on national television. But the best thing about Granny was her stories. Every night, before bed, they would snuggle around her on the sofa and she would tell them a tale.

'I want to tell you a story about three very dear friends of mine,' began Grandmother on the first night of their visit, 'Nathan, Gerald and Sophie.' She dabbed a tear away from her eye.

'Why are you crying, Grandmother?' asked Peter.

'I can't tell you, it would ruin the story,' said Grandmother.

'Is it a sad story?' asked Luke.

'In parts,' admitted Grandmother. 'When I think of how those poor pigs suffered . . . ' Grandmother said no more, she just sniffed.

'The story is about pigs?' asked Lucy.

'That's what I said,' said Grandmother. 'Nathan, Gerald and Sophie.'

'You didn't say they were pigs,' said Peter.

'I don't know why you would assume they *weren't* pigs,' said Grandmother. 'My story is about three young people, who just happened to be pigs, whose cruel mother forced them to go out and find their own places to live'.

'She made them leave home when they were just children?!' exclaimed Lucy.

'No, they were in their early thirties,' said Grandmother, 'but it's cruel to force a child to leave home when you are good at cooking. If you can make a caramel basket as delicious as the ones my friend Madge whips up, you can understand why it is cruel to expect her children to go and live anywhere else. But still, you don't get to be that good at caramelising sugar without hardening your heart (whenever I try to do it, I find it impossible to resist eating the sugar straight out of the bag before I even get started). So one day, after being given two months' notice and plenty of money to pay for a rental bond each, Madge forced her children heartlessly into the street.'

'If they had money for a rental bond, what was the problem?' asked Peter. 'Why didn't they just rent a flat?'

'Because they were pigs,' said Grandmother, as though that explained everything.

The children looked confused.

'They took the bond money straight around to

the sweet shop, spent it all on lollies and sat on the gutter outside the shop eating them all afternoon,' explained Grandmother.

'That's appalling!' said Lucy.

'I know,' said Grandmother. 'It is all very well to sit in the gutter if you want to weep in despair, or if your shoes are dirty and you need to wash them off in rain water. But if you are going to eat lollies it is much better to sit underneath a bush. Then you are much less likely to be interrupted by someone wanting to share with you.'

'No, I meant it is appalling for them to spend all the rent money on lollies,' said Lucy.

Now Grandmother looked confused. 'But what else could they do? If you are going to be homeless it is important to be well fed.'

Lucy was about to argue further, but Peter touched her hand and shook his head ever so slightly. There was no way Grandmother would ever see reason in an argument against eating dangerously huge amounts of sugary foods.

'So having had a lovely little snack, the three young pigs set off to find somewhere to live,' continued Grandmother. 'Of course they could not live together.'

'Why not?' asked Luke.

'Because they were brothers and sister,' said Grandmother. 'So naturally they fought terribly.'

'But we're brothers and sister,' said Peter, 'and we don't fight terribly.'

'Yes, but that is because you have my mature guiding influence,' said Grandmother.

'You get into fights all the time,' Luke pointed out.

'Exactly,' said Grandmother, 'which saves you having to fight, which is why you can get along so peaceably together. Anyway, Nathan, Gerald and Sophie were not as lucky as you. They bickered. So as they set off down the road they were looking for three separate places to live.'

'Let me guess,' said Peter. 'Nathan built a house of straw.'

'How did you know?!' asked Grandmother, taken aback.

'I've heard a similar story before,' admitted Peter.

'Well, you haven't got it quite right,' said Grandmother. 'He didn't build his house of straw. He built it of drinking straws.'

'What?' said Luke (rudely because, as you know, you should always say 'I beg your pardon,' but he was so shocked he forgot his manners).

'You see Nathan could not afford to buy any straw, being penniless, but he could go around to all the fast food establishments, milk bars and sandwich shops in town and, when nobody was looking, take three or four straws from their dispensers. It took him several months. But eventually he had enough drinking straws to build a two-bedroom bungalow with a rumpus room and an entertaining deck,' said Grandmother.

'He built an entire house out of drinking straws?' marvelled Peter.

'Yes, it was jolly good fun actually,' said Grandmother. 'True, they did crackle a bit under foot as you walked about, but you could run and bounce into the walls like a bouncy castle. And the walls were made with bending straws, so you could lower the ceiling when you needed to change a light bulb.'

Grandmother stopped at this point and started eating cake.

'Aren't you going to tell us the rest of the story?' asked Lucy.

'What was wrong with that story?' asked Grandmother. 'It had a happy ending and taught you an important lesson about recycling and using sustainable materials to build a dwelling.'

'Technically I don't think it is recycling unless the straws had been used for drinking first,' said Luke.

'Well, that would have been disgustingly unhygienic,' said Grandmother.

'But what about Gerald and Sophie?' asked Lucy.

'You want to know about them too?' asked Grandmother.

'Yes,' said all three children (this was by far the most intriguing version of the three little pigs they had ever heard).

'Gerald was not as good at lateral thinking as his brother or sister, so as he walked along the road it did not occur to him to use drinking straws, drinking cups or any other disposable beverage aid to build a house. Night fell and he had nowhere to stay,' said Grandmother.

'That's terrible,' said Lucy.

'Not really,' disagreed Grandmother. 'It was summer, and therefore a warm night. He just lay down under a tree, took the lolly wrappers out of his pockets and sprinkled them all over himself as a makeshift blanket, and fell asleep quite happily.'

'So he didn't build a house?' asked Luke.

'Oh yes, he did,' said Grandmother, 'because the next morning Mother Nature had given him a brilliant idea.'

'Mother Nature?' asked Luke.

'Yes, when he woke up in the morning a branch had fallen on him,' said Grandmother. 'He was covered in sticks!'

'And that gave him the idea to make a house out of sticks?' guessed Peter.

'No,' said Grandmother, 'although, now you mention it, that's not a bad idea. No, it gave him the idea to make a house of matchsticks!'

'What?' said all three children (they were all so enthralled in the story, they had lost their manners).

'But how?' asked Lucy, totally baffled.

'He was a natural scavenger like his brother,' explained Grandmother, 'so he went around to bars and restaurants—anywhere that gave away free matchboxes.'

'It must have taken him forever to build a house out of all those teeny tiny sticks,' marvelled Peter.

'Oh yes,' agreed Grandmother. 'And an absolute ocean of model glue.'

'How could he afford to buy the glue?' asked Lucy.

'He got lucky there,' admitted Grandmother. 'A glue truck crashed at the end of his street, so he was able to scavenge vats and vats full. And that's how he built his house of matchsticks.'

'So how did Sophie build her house?' asked Luke.

'Ahah,' said Grandmother. 'She was a far more sensible pig than her brothers and she had something of her mother's genius for desserts.

So she did not build her house of drinking straws or matchsticks, she built her house entirely out of chocolate.'

'Wow!' said all three children.

'But surely it would melt?' said Peter. 'You said it was summer?'

'She had huge outdoor air-conditioners set up to blast cold air at the house,' explained Grandmother, 'and a giant parasol overhead to block the sunlight.'

'But where did she get the chocolate from if she didn't have any money?' asked Lucy.

'Pillow mints,' said Grandmother.

'Pillow mints?' asked the children.

'Yes, if you stay in a fancy hotel, they often put a chocolate mint on your pillow when they make your bed,' said Grandmother. 'It's to encourage tooth decay, by luring you into eating chocolate after you've brushed your teeth.'

'But how did she get enough pillow mints to build a house?' asked Luke.

'By going through the trash of course,' said Grandmother. 'I know it is hard to believe, but some people who stay in fancy hotels—people like dentists, diabetics and dieters—they do not eat their pillow mints.'

'And they throw them away?' asked Peter.

'They do,' concurred Grandmother. 'Shocking isn't it? So by going around to all the hotels in the city and gathering up all the unwanted pillow mints, Sophie was able to get enough chocolate to build her home.'

'And what happened next?' asked Lucy.

'Isn't that enough?' asked Grandmother. 'I tell you three extraordinary stories of pigs exhibiting unparalleled resourcefulness and architectural ingenuity and you want more?!'

'What happened to the house?' asked Peter. 'Wasn't there a wolf?'

'No,' said Grandmother. 'Whatever gave you that idea?'

'So all three houses are still standing?' asked Luke. 'No one blew them down?'

'Oh I didn't say that,' said Grandmother. 'There was a wicked butcher, called Mr Wolf.'

'Was he a wolf?' asked Lucy.

'No,' said Grandmother. 'Whatever would make you think that? He was a human called Wolf. Do I need to slow down or write out some notes for you because you're finding it hard to follow?'

'No, just keep telling the story,' pleaded Peter.

‘Well this wicked butcher was too cheap and mean to actually pay for meat,’ said Grandmother. ‘He would never buy beef, lamb or pork from a farmer. He would scavenge for meat.’

‘But how can you scavenge for beef?’ asked Peter.‘You don’t find cows lying about the place.’

‘Exactly,’ said Grandmother. ‘He would pick up possums and cats and pigeons that had been hit by cars and were lying dead on the side of the road, take them back to his shop, cut them up and stick them under signs saying they were beef or pork or lamb.’

‘That’s dreadful!’ exclaimed Lucy.

‘But how did he get away with it?’ asked Peter. ‘Possum or cat wouldn’t taste like lamb or beef.’

‘It would if you covered it in peanut sauce and called it a satay stick!’ declared Grandmother.

The children gasped.

‘That’s right,’ continued Grandmother. ‘You should always be sure of the motives of your butcher before you buy any of his pre-prepared ready-sauced foods.’

‘I think I’m going to be sick,’ said Peter.

‘So you can just imagine what such a wicked man thought when he heard that there were three young pigs living alone in the woods,’ said Grandmother.

'He thought he could sell them some cat meat?' guessed Luke.

'No, silly,' said Peter. 'He wanted to chop them up.'

'He did indeed,' declared Grandmother. 'He picked up his sharpest butcher knife and set off into the woods. It was not long before he came to the house of straws.'

'Did he knock on the door?' asked Luke.

'He did,' said Grandmother, 'But it doesn't make much noise when you knock on a door made out of drinking straws, so he had to yell, "Little pig, little pig, open the door or I'll knock it down by force." And Nathan replied, "Never, I won't let you chop me up and cover me in sweet and sour sauce."'

'Well as you can imagine, a fully grown butcher with a very sharp knife was never going to be delayed for long by a door made out of drinking straws. The special in his butcher shop that week was pork in plum sauce,' said Grandmother.

'That's dreadful!' exclaimed Lucy.

'I know,' agreed Grandmother, 'and the customers so enjoyed eating actual pork that he soon sold out. So the butcher went back into the woods in search of the second pig.'

'I don't like the way this is going,' said Luke.

'He soon came to the house of matchsticks,' said Grandmother, 'but again the little pig refused to let him in.'

'So did he hack the door down with his meat cleaver?' asked Peter.

'He tried,' said Grandmother, 'but the second little pig was actually quite a gifted model-maker. He had used so much glue that, when the butcher made his first hack, the knife got stuck in the door and he couldn't pull it out.'

'So the little pig was saved?' asked Lucy.

'He would have been,' said Grandmother, 'but unfortunately the butcher was so frustrated he stamped and stomped on the ground, then he kicked at the dirt and inadvertently kicked a stone at the house. That stone was made of flint and when it hit the house it caused a spark.'

'Oh dear,' said Peter, guessing what was coming next.

'When you make a house of matchsticks and highly flammable hobby glue you don't want sparks coming anywhere near your home,' said Grandmother. 'The butcher had Cajun pork on special that week.

'When all the slightly burnt pork was sold, the

butcher set out into the woods in search of the third pig, and that is when he came to the house of chocolate,' said Grandmother.

'And he couldn't get in because the house was so well made?' guessed Luke.

'No, the third little pig invited him in,' said Grandmother. "'Little pig, little pig, let me come in," cried the butcher. And surprisingly Sophie replied,

"Sure but I've lost the key to the front door, so you'll have to eat your way in."

'The butcher enjoyed chocolate as much as the next person, so he put down his knife and started chomping,' said Grandmother. 'Little did he know that Sophie was a deeply sensible pig. Her front door was not like a common house door, which is only two inches thick. She had made her solid chocolate door two *feet* thick. So the butcher ate and ate, and ate and ate, but he had to eat 50 kilos of chocolate before he broke through, and another 90 kilos of chocolate before there was a hole big enough for him to climb through. And by the time he had eaten the 140 kilos of chocolate he wasn't capable of climbing anywhere. He just lay on the ground moaning.'

'Is that the end of the story?' asked Lucy.

'Pretty much,' said Grandmother.

'So the butcher learnt his lesson,' guessed Peter, 'and never troubled Sophie again.'

'In a way,' agreed Grandmother. 'While Sophie had endured a lifetime of bickering and fighting with her brothers she did still love them. So she was not going to let the butcher off that easily.'

'So what happened?' asked Luke.

'Sophie decided she would run the butcher shop,' said Grandmother, 'and that week's special was Mr Wolf Pie. All the customers assumed that Mr Wolf had made the pie. Little did they realise that he had been made *into* the pie.'

The children stared at Grandmother in stunned silence.

'And so Sophie lived happily ever after, and to this day she runs the best vegetarian butcher shop in all the land. The end,' said Grandmother. 'Now, time for bed.'

CHOOSE YOUR OWN ADVENTURE

by

John Marsden

CHAPTER 1

The phone rings. You grab it out of the kitchen sink and shake the onion skin off it.

It's Captain Cook on the other end.

'Listen,' he says, 'you interested in taking a trip? I'm going to discover Australia, leaving tomorrow. You want to come?'

If you say 'yes', go to chapter 2. If you say 'no', go to chapter 3.

▲ ▲ ▲

CHAPTER 2

'Sure,' you say. 'I'll just ask my mum.' You put the phone on mute. 'Mum,' you yell, 'Captain Cook's on the phone. Is it okay if I go and help discover Australia?'

'How long will you be?' she yells back.

'I don't know. About six months, I guess.'

'All right. You better take your bathers, though, in case there's a beach. They're in the dryer.'

You tell Captain Cook, 'I'm there. Meet you at the dock.'

'Good. Now, we've only got two vacancies left. Do you want to be the chef or the lookout? You'd better decide now, because there's this Sir Joseph Banks guy and he'll take the other spot.'

Yikes, you think. The chef has a lot of work and if the sailors don't like the food they could get pretty upset. On the other hand, the chef stays warm and dry, and never goes hungry. The lookout has to climb those tall masts, but it's a great view from up there.

If you say 'chef' go to chapter 4. If you say 'lookout', go to chapter 5.

▲ ▲ ▲

CHAPTER 3

'No way,' you tell the captain. 'There could be anything out there. Crocodiles and sharks and lamingtons and snakes.'

'It's true, lamingtons do sound dangerous,' he admits.

'Excuse me, but I'm right in the middle of

US Marines Versus Everybody Else 3. Find some other sucker,' you say, and terminate the call.

Little do you realise you've just turned down the chance to be famous, have towns and rivers named after you, and have kids do assignments on you at school. Bummer!

THE END

▲ ▲ ▲

CHAPTER 4

'I'll take chef,' you say.

'Good choice,' he says, although you get the feeling he says that to everyone, just to encourage them. 'You'd better pick up a few slabs of Coke on your way down to the wharf. It's a long trip, and we'll need all the Coke we can get.'

'Why?' you ask.

'There's nothing better for cleaning the saucepans,' he explains. 'Gets rid of grease and stains and spots. Great stuff.'

Next day you set sail. Before long you're heading around the Cape of Good Hope. However, your cooking is hopeless, and the sailors have become suspicious of your chicken nuggets.

'We never had any chickens on board,' they tell you.

'So?'

'But we did have a lot of rats running around when we left England.'

'So what?'

'Now there are no rats left.'

'Is that right? Oh, by the way, I'm taking chicken nuggets off the menu, guys. Sorry.'

They complain to Captain Cook. 'Throw the cook overboard!' they yell.

'Throw me overboard?' Captain Cook says, looking surprised. 'But I've given you everything you wanted. Free Wi-Fi, cable TV, 24-hour childcare . . .'

But by now, the sailors are overexcited. They're determined to throw someone overboard.

If they throw Captain Cook overboard, go to chapter 6. If they throw you overboard, go to chapter 7.

▲ ▲ ▲

CHAPTER 5

'I'll take lookout,' you say.

'Good choice,' he says, although you get the

feeling he says that to everyone, just to encourage them. 'Are you a good climber?'

'Oh, not bad,' you say.

'You'd better bring your undies. Otherwise the crew can see up your trouser legs.'

Charming, you think.

Two days into the voyage you get to climb the mast for the first time. The higher you go, the scarier it gets. The mast sways from side to side, and with a strong breeze blowing you feel like you're climbing a kite string. Miles below on the deck stands the boatswain, Sydney Codswallop, a man you've already learned to hate.

'Get a move on, landlubber!' he yells. 'Shift your butt, you lazy bag of blubber! Work those legs, spindleshanks. Oh, and by the way, nice undies.'

You grit your teeth and climb on. But the mast is slippery and you're getting tired. The swaying makes you dizzy and you realise you're in imminent danger of crashing to the deck far below, and breaking every bone in your body.

If you get to the top, go to chapter 9. If you fall, go to chapter 10.

▲ ▲ ▲

CHAPTER 6

They grab Captain Cook, and chuck him off the bridge. He splashes into the ocean. There is a sudden boiling of water and blood and you see a whole bunch of sharks swimming away in different directions. They all have bits of Captain Cook in their mouths.

'What have you done?' you yell at the crew. 'Morons! Turn the boat around. We'll have to go home. We can't discover Australia now.'

'Why not?' they ask, looking disappointed.

'Haven't you read the history books?' you ask them. 'Without Captain Cook, the indigenous people get to keep Australia. We're stuck with life in England. Rain, traffic jams, cricket matches, Marmite! Good on you guys!'

THE END

▲ ▲ ▲

CHAPTER 7

They grab you and hurl you into the ocean. And the bad news is that there is no police-rescue helicopter. You thrash around, trying to remember whether you can swim or not. In the distance you see the fins of sharks. The fins are as big as the sails on the ship. These sharks have been following the ship for weeks. It could be because of all the food you threw overboard. The food that the crew would not eat.

If you stay in the water with the sharks, go to chapter 8. If you get back on the ship, go to chapter 11.

▲ ▲ ▲

CHAPTER 8

Dear reader, you are a very sick person. I know you only chose this option because you wanted lots of blood and gore as the sharks tear you to pieces. You wanted a sickening description of torn limbs, shredded intestines, bleeding eyeballs, minced limbs, and severed fingers. Horrified screams, followed by blood gurgling in your throat as you feel your body ripped apart. A decapitated head bobbing around in the waves . . .

Well, I am not going to pander to your grotesque tastes. You've been watching too many *Simpsons* Halloween episodes. This is going to be a happy ending.

You see the sharks swimming towards you. You expect the worst. You're sweating so much that the ocean rises around you, with the extra water. The sharks reach you.

They're smiling! Their huge white teeth gleam at you. 'Loved those chicken nuggets,' they say. 'Any more of those?'

'Sorry, we're fresh out of rats,' you say. 'But I can do a nice fish finger. Just bring me some fish. Or some fingers. Or sea slugs will do. Anything really.'

They take you away with them to their ocean kingdom, where you live happily ever after, preparing delicious meals for your new family.

THE END

▲ ▲ ▲

CHAPTER 9

With arms and legs trembling and your brain feeling like melted butter you make it to the top. Rather than risk that again, you stay there for the rest of the trip. Luckily, the chef agrees to send your meals up to you. As for going to the toilet . . . Well, we won't go into that, except to say that people on the deck below soon learn to carry umbrellas.

At last comes the memorable day when you see a dark shape on the horizon, and this time you know it's not a cloud bank.

'Australia!' you shout excitedly to Boatswain Sydney Codswallop and Captain Cook and everybody else.

They run to the bow and stare. Then they walk away again.

'You ludicrous excuse for a lookout's tapeworm! Clean your glasses,' the boatswain yells at you. Embarrassed, you take off your sunnies, clean them, then put them back on again. The dark shape on the horizon has disappeared. Amazing what a smudge on your glasses can do.

However, three weeks later, you see an even bigger shape, and this time there's no mistake. Excitement mounts as the ship gets closer. The crew has a competition to name the place you're approaching. The boatswain agrees to be judge. The winner is the acting deputy assistant junior flag-folder, who has a bit of spare time, and comes up with the answer of Sydney. By a strange coincidence, that's the boatswain's name.

Soon you're there, sailing past the Opera House and under the Harbour Bridge. You look at everything, trying to take it all in. Just think, in about 160 years, cars will start driving across that bridge, and 40 years after that someone will be singing *Waltzing Matilda* in the Opera House.

Well, now that you've discovered Australia, it's off to the airport to fly home. You say farewell to Captain Cook, warning him never to go near the Sandwich Islands, especially in 1779, because he might just get a spear through his brisket. He doesn't seem to be paying much attention, though. You wave goodbye to the crew and set off to the airport. You're looking forward to a good choice of movies on the plane.

THE END

▲ ▲ ▲

CHAPTER 10

Your shoulders are hurting and your arms are aching. Somehow, no matter how hard you try and how much you sweat, you can't make any progress. In the last two or three minutes you've only gained 50 centimetres. Then you lose your grip and in an instant you're plummeting through space. Way below, Boatswain Codswallop stands looking up at you. His mouth is open in shock and horror. Your life flashes before your eyes. Being chased by the boa constrictor that escaped from the zoo, cleaning your teeth with your brother's shaving cream, lying on the road after the gelato van ran you over, struggling to beat your Chupa Chups addiction, returning your overdue copy of *Hop on Pop* to the fearsome Ms Burroughs in the library . . . Wow, it's a wonder you got to live this long! You've had nine lives already!

You hit the deck so hard you smash straight through it. You keep going, through the galley. The chef waves to you. Hey, you could have had that job. You smash on through Captain Cook's cabin, through the cargo hold, through the bottom of the boat. Boy, that was some fall. At last, you hit the ocean floor. You look around. Right next to you is a huge shape, overgrown with barnacles and crawling with crabs. You recognise it. It's the Titanic! Wait a minute! The Titanic sailed in 1912. And Captain Cook sailed in 1770. What's going on here? How can you be looking at the Titanic 142 years before it sinks?

You thought life was weird. But death's even weirder. Interesting.

THE END

▲ ▲ ▲

CHAPTER 11

The sight of the sharks motivates you, and you suddenly remember that you won the 100-metre freestyle bronze medal at the last Olympics. You get to the ship in a personal best of 52.4 seconds. The crew are so impressed they let you back on board.

You take a bit more care with the food. From now on, you serve French fries to everyone. Luckily the supply of French lasts until you get to Australia.

At last you reach Port Jackson. You get off the ship into a lifeboat, and row ashore. You get quite a shock when you land. There's a whole bunch of Aboriginal people standing there looking at you.

'What do you think you're doing?' they ask.

'We're finding Australia,' you explain.

'You idiots! We never lost it in the first place!' they tell you.

You feel really stupid. 'Sorry,' you say.

They sigh. 'Now you say sorry?' one of them says. They all turn and walk away.

Captain Cook appears on your left. 'Check this out!' he calls excitedly.

You go over to him. ‘Look,’ he says. ‘I’ve found the perfect place for a multi-storey car park. We’ll just chop down a couple of thousand gum trees, get rid of the koalas and wombats and start building. Let’s go!’

He picks up an axe. You stand there thinking, *Maybe this wasn’t such a good idea*.

THE END

THE HALLOWEEN CHICKEN

by

Alex Ratt

Tracey woke up in a bad mood. The next day was Halloween, and she knew from previous Halloweens that until it was over her life would be a misery.

Stanley Blotson, who sat behind her at school, had been playing pranks all week, trying to scare her so he could say: 'What are you, a *chicken*? Yes! That's exactly what you are!'

And: 'Tracey's a *chicken*!'

Then he'd bray with laughter: 'Hee haw! Hee haw! Hee haw!'

Tracey pulled on her school uniform and stomped down the stairs to the kitchen. Her dad was standing by the bench with a slice of toast.

'Hey there, chickadee,' he said.

'Hi, Dad,' she said.

'You're looking glum,' he noted. 'Everything okay?'

'Not really,' Tracey began. 'Everyone's making fun of me because—'

But before Tracey could finish, her dad's phone began to cluck like a chicken.

Her dad laughed delightedly. 'Isn't my new ringtone great?'

Tracey groaned.

'Sorry, Trace—work call. Got to take this.' He pressed a button then put the phone to his ear. 'Charlie Chicken's Plumbing Repairs. Charlie Chicken speaking.'

He listened for a few moments then said, 'A blocked toilet? No worries. We Chickens aren't afraid of getting our hands dirty. *Chickens aren't afraid*—get it?' He winked at Tracey.

Tracey groaned again. There was no point complaining to her dad about how she was being tormented at school because of her surname. He thought being a Chicken was great!

As Tracey filled her bowl with cereal, her dad started telling stories about the things he'd found blocking toilets. It was a relief when he said, 'Hang on, I'll check my appointment book,' and left the kitchen; his stories were putting Tracey off her breakfast.

As her dad exited, Tracey's big sister Stacey entered.

'What's your problem?' said Stacey before Tracey could say a word.

'I'm glad you asked,' said Tracey. Surely her sister would sympathise. She was probably going through the same thing herself. 'It's Stanley Blotson. He's been scaring me with stupid Halloween pranks all week, just so he can call me a chicken when I scream.'

Stacey rolled her eyes. 'Number one,' she said, 'when I asked what your problem was I didn't really want an answer. What I meant was: get out of my way, numbskull.' She pushed Tracey aside and headed for the fridge. 'And number two, primary school is *so* childish. I'm sure your little friend will grow out of it when he gets to high school.' Ever since she'd started high school herself, Stacey had been acting like she was ten years older than Tracey instead of two.

'Stanley Blotson is *not* my friend,' Tracey muttered as Stacey took an apple from the crisper.

When her sister was gone, Tracey poured milk over her Crispy Crunchy Crackles and carried the bowl to the table. She'd just sat down when her mum rushed in. 'Didn't you have a form for me to sign about that excursion next week?' she asked.

'I have to leave for work in 20 seconds so if you want it signed now's the time.'

'Oh yeah.' Tracey ran upstairs to look for the form at the bottom of her schoolbag, but it must have taken her longer than 20 seconds to find it, because when she returned her mum was gone.

And so was all the milk from her cereal bowl. There was just a heap of Not-So-Crispy Crunchy Crackles.

'Who took my milk?' Tracey called.

There was no answer.

'That's a pretty *childish* prank, Stacey.'

Still no answer.

Great, she thought. Now she had to worry about pranks at home as well as school.

▲ ▲ ▲

As she walked through the school gate that morning, Tracey was hoping that Stanley Blotson was away sick that day. But she was out of luck, because as she walked towards the classroom he came running over. 'Hey, are you excited about Halloween tomorrow? Oh no, that's right, I forgot: you're a *chicken*! Hee haw!'

The day was every bit as bad as Tracey had anticipated.

When she pulled her maths book from under her desk an enormous spider fell into her lap.

'Eek!' Tracey shrieked.

'Hee haw!' brayed Stanley. 'It's only a fake spider! You're such a chicken, Chicken!'

When Tracey reached for the orange paint during art class, Stanley snatched it from her hand.

'Hey, give that back,' said Tracey.

She turned around to take it from him and saw to her horror that Stanley's face had started to melt.

'Eek!' said Tracey.

'Hee haw!' brayed Stanley. 'It's only a mask. What a *chicken*!'

And when Tracey sat down at her desk after lunch she let out a big long *paaaaaaaaarrrrrp*.

Stanley had put a whoopee cushion on her seat.

'That wasn't even scary,' she snapped as everyone laughed.

'It was for the people sitting behind you!' said Stanley. 'Hee haw! Hee haw!'

As they walked towards the school gate at the end of the day, Stanley said, 'Just you wait, Chicken; tomorrow will be even more fun.'

Even more fun . . . Tracey walked home from school dreading the thought of what the next day would bring.

'Hard day at school?' her mum said sympathetically when Tracey entered the kitchen. She was sitting at the table with a steaming pot of tea.

'The worst,' said Tracey. Then she remembered

Stanley's warning. 'Or maybe only the second-worst,' she said gloomily.

'That's a shame,' said her mum. She picked up the milk jug and started to pour, but nothing came out. 'Hey,' she said, peering into the jug. 'Where did my milk go?'

'Ask Stacey,' Tracey said, and she went upstairs to change.

▲ ▲ ▲

Tracey was tense that evening. She felt nervous about what Stanley had planned for the next day. When her dad said after dinner, 'Come on, Trace—let's watch scary movies to get ourselves in the Halloween spirit,' Tracey shook her head.

'No, thanks,' she said. 'I'm already dreading tomorrow. I'm going to my room to read.'

'Aw, Trace, don't be such a chicken,' her dad said, then laughed. 'Get it? Don't be a chicken . . . you *are* a Chicken!'

'Yeah, Dad, I get it.'

'How about some dessert?' her mum offered. 'It's pumpkin pie. Because nothing says "Halloween" like pumpkins, right?'

Tracey wasn't interested in anything that said 'Halloween'. 'I'm just going to have some cereal,' she said, and fixed herself a big bowl of Crispy Crunchy Crackles.

Sitting up in bed with her bowl of cereal and a comic book, Tracey finally began to relax.

She had reached a particularly exciting scene, in which Amazing Alice was about to battle a giant serpent, when she found the pages of her comic were stuck together.

Tracey put her cereal bowl on the floor and prised the pages apart, then reached down to pick up the bowl again.

Still reading, she lifted the spoon to her mouth, then looked down at the bowl. There was no milk left. Weird. There was no way Stacey could have done it . . . unless she was hiding under the bed!

Leaning over the side of the mattress, Tracey thrust her arm under the bed and flailed it about, hoping to strike her sister. 'I know you're there,' she said.

Then: 'Ow!'

Yanking her hand back, she stared in disbelief at the two small punctures on her finger. Something had bitten her! Something with . . . fangs. And while Stacey was a snake, she didn't have fangs.

Suddenly it all fell into place. It wasn't Stacey who had been causing the milk to disappear—it WAS a snake! Snakes loved milk. Snakes had fangs. There was a snake in the house! And not just in the house—under her bed!

Could Stanley have let a snake loose in her bedroom?

Heart pounding, she peered over the edge of the bed.

There she saw the glint of black beady eyes.

'*Snake!*' Tracey scooted backwards until she was pressed against the wall. 'Mum!' she squeaked.

A peal of laughter rose from downstairs. Clearly the movie was not that scary.

'Dad!'

Chortles and snorts wafted up.

'Stacey!'

A series of high-pitched giggles.

Brilliant. While her family was downstairs watching a so-called scary movie, she was living a real-life horror film, trapped in her room with a snake.

There was a rustling, and then something began

to emerge from beneath the bed. Too scared even to cry out, Tracey watched in terror.

First, a twitching nose.

(*Do snakes even have noses?* Tracey wondered.)

Then a cute little furry face.

(*What kind of snake has a cute little furry face?*)

And then a round spiky body.

(*A round spiky—?*)

'Hang on!' Tracey said aloud. 'You're not a snake.'

The creature turned to look at her. 'Of course I am not a snake,' it said. 'I am Count Hedgehogula!'

'You're *what*?' said Tracey.

'Count Hedgehogula,' it repeated.

'So you're a hedgehog?'

'I am a vampire!' said the creature.

'You look more like a hedgehog.'

'Have you ever seen a hedgehog with teeth like this?' The hedgehog grimaced and Tracey yelped at the sight of its gleaming fangs.

'Okay, you really are a vampire. Do you . . . do you want to drink my blood now?'

'Blood?' said the vampire hedgehog. 'No! Yuck. I want to drink your milk.'

'What are you doing here?' Tracey asked. 'Did

Stanley Blotson have something to do with it? Are you some kind of Halloween prank?'

'How dare you!' sputtered the hedgehog. 'I am no "prank". I come from a noble family with a castle in Transylvania.'

'Like Count Dracula?'

The hedgehog frowned. 'Never heard of him.'

'But how did you get here?' Tracey asked.

The hedgehog thought for a minute. 'I can't remember. I think I stowed away.'

'Are you lost?'

'I suppose so,' said the hedgehog vaguely.

'I'll help you find your way home tomorrow,' said Tracey. 'It's bedtime now.'

She went to the bathroom and brushed her teeth, called 'goodnight' down the stairs, and changed into her pyjamas.

'Goodnight, Count Hedgehogula,' she said as she switched off the bedside lamp.

'Sweet dreams,' said the vampire.

▲ ▲ ▲

The next morning, instead of feeling a sense of doom, Tracey woke up laughing at the strange dream she'd had. A vampire hedgehog! She'd never heard anything so crazy.

But as she was getting dressed she heard a small voice say from under the bed, 'I want to drink your milk!'

'You mean you're real?' Tracey said, bending down to look under the bed.

A pair of beady eyes blinked back at her.

'I'm sorry,' Tracey said, 'but I won't be able to help you find your way home till after school.'

'I want some more of that special milk,' said the hedgehog. 'What makes it taste so good?'

'It's cereal milk,' Tracey explained.

She went downstairs and made two bowls of Crispy Crunchy Crackles, then she carried one upstairs and put it under the bed.

▲ ▲ ▲

It was only as she was walking to school that she remembered she still had to face Halloween with Stanley Blotson. If he wasn't responsible for putting a vampire hedgehog under her bed, that meant he had some other devious trick planned.

But the morning passed quietly. Once Stanley jumped out from behind a door and yelled 'Boo!', but Tracey had seen him hiding in the first place and so she hardly even flinched.

She'd almost forgotten it was Halloween when

she put her hand under her desk to get her ruler and something brushed against her fingers.

Tracey flung herself back in her seat. 'Ms Handel,' she called, 'I think there's something under my desk.'

Ms Handel frowned. 'I should think there are lots of things under your desk, Tracey,' she said.

'I meant something *alive*,' Tracey clarified.

'Oh,' said Ms Handel, coming over. 'That's another story.'

'I saw something!' said Stanley, who was standing behind them. 'Oh no! Here it comes!'

Suddenly, a snake shot out from under the desk!

'SNAKE!' yelled Ms Handel.

But out of the corner of her eye, Tracey had seen Stanley jerk his hand as the snake came flying out.

'That's just a rubber snake tied to a fishing line,' she said accusingly.

Ms Handel whirled around. 'Stanley,' she scolded. 'That's a terrible trick. I want you to stay behind after school and write *I will not hide rubber snakes under my classmates' desks* 50 times.'

'Hmph,' said Stanley. 'You're no fun, Chicken.'

'Thank you,' said Tracey.

'It's rather hot in here,' Ms Handel said, fanning

herself. She still looked a bit flustered. 'Class, we're going out to the oval to play hacky sack.'

After several rounds of hacky sack, which allowed Ms Handel to blow her whistle until she wasn't flustered any more, the teacher glanced at her watch and said, 'Tracey, can you fetch the lunch orders, please?'

Tracey went to the canteen and fetched the basket with the lunch orders, carried it back to the classroom and then returned to the oval.

The bell rang just as she got there, so they all trooped back to class.

'Hey, what happened to my chocolate milk?' Stanley demanded when he pulled his lunch order from the basket. 'The carton is empty.'

'Maybe you already drank it,' said Ryan.

'How could I have drunk it? I only just got here. Was it you, Chicken?'

Tracey looked at the milk he was holding. 'How could I have drunk it?' she said. 'The carton hasn't been opened.'

Stanley stared at it, puzzled. 'Then how did the milk get out?'

Another mystery of missing milk . . . Was it possible?

'Are there fang marks in the carton?' Tracey asked.

'Fang marks?' said Stanley. 'Don't be stupid, of course there are no . . . oh. Um, there are some f-fang marks.'

There was a slight tremor in his voice, Tracey noticed. Could Stanley Blotson be scared?

'You know who likes milk, don't you?' she said casually. 'Snakes.'

Stanley turned so pale it looked as if his blood had been drained by a real vampire.

'Y-y-you mean like a r-r-real s-s-snake?' Stanley looked around wildly.

'That's right,' said Tracey. 'There must be a snake in here. You're not *chicken*, are you?'

'SNAKE!' Stanley yelled. 'THERE'S A SNAKE IN THE CLASSROOM! SNAKE!'

Everyone stampeded from the room.

Tracey followed them to the door, then closed it behind them.

'What are you doing in there, Tracey?' the teacher called from the other side of the door.

'Don't worry, Ms Handel. I know how to deal with snakes.' Turning back to face the room, Tracey called softly, 'Count Hedgehogula, are you in here?'

There was no reply, and for a few dreadful

moments Tracey feared that she had made a terrible mistake. Maybe there really was a snake in here!

Then a voice said, 'That milk—it was *so* tasty.'

The vampire hedgehog waddled out from behind the wastepaper bin, chocolate milk dripping from its fangs.

'What are you doing here?' said Tracey.

'I don't know. I drank the special milk this morning and it made me very sleepy—vampires usually sleep during the day, you know. So I found a cosy place to rest, and when I woke up I was here—and I could smell the most delicious milk. What was it?'

'Chocolate milk,' said Tracey. 'And that cosy place must have been my schoolbag.'

'And are there more special milks like this at your school?'

'Sure,' said Tracey. 'There's strawberry, banana . . . lots of different flavours.'

'I would like to try them all,' said the hedgehog. 'But now I am sleepy again.'

'You can have a sleep in a minute,' said Tracey, 'but first I want you to do me a favour. Get back in my schoolbag, and when I give it a shake I want you to wriggle and hiss.'

'Why should I do this?'

‘Because there’s a horrid boy who thinks you’re a snake, and if I can scare him maybe he’ll stop scaring me.’

‘I see,’ said Count Hedgehogula. ‘Very well. Since you have been so kind, I will help you.’

Just then there was an urgent knocking at the door accompanied by Ms Handel’s panicked voice. ‘Tracey, are you all right in there? Who are you talking to?’

‘Coming,’ Tracey called. ‘I was just soothing the snake.’

She opened her schoolbag and the hedgehog crawled inside.

‘Okay, I’m coming out now.’ Tracey opened the door to find the whole class crowded into the corridor.

‘Give me room,’ Tracey said, brandishing the bag. ‘It’s a big one.’

She gave the bag a little shake and the hedgehog squirmed and hissed obediently.

Everyone screamed; Stanley Blotson screamed loudest of all.

‘I found it under Stanley’s desk.’ She moved towards Stanley and he whimpered and flattened himself against the wall of the corridor.

‘It must have come from the nature reserve that backs onto the oval,’ Tracey continued. ‘I’m going to take it back there and release it.’

Tracey carried her bag across the oval to the edge of the bushland. There she crouched down and opened her bag. ‘Wait under this bush for a couple of hours and I’ll come back and fetch you after school,’ she told the hedgehog.

The hedgehog curled into a ball. ‘Very well,’ he murmured. ‘In the meantime, I will have a short rest and contemplate all the special milks I am yet to try.’

When Tracey returned to the classroom, everyone cheered.

▲ ▲ ▲

After school, Tracey walked back across the oval to find Count Hedgehogula fast asleep under the bush where she’d left him. She picked him up very gently so as not to wake him (and so as not to hurt her hand on the prickles) and put him back into her schoolbag.

Back in her room at home she removed him. He stretched and yawned and looked around, nose twitching. ‘We are home,’ he said.

'Well, my home, not yours. We need to get you back to Transylvania. Have you remembered how you got here?'

The hedgehog tilted his head to one side. 'It doesn't matter—I have decided to stay here with you. We have no special milk in Transylvania.'

'I don't know,' Tracey said doubtfully. She was reluctant to share her room with a vampire, even if he only wanted to drink her milk.

Then she remembered what Stanley Blotson had said when she returned from the oval after releasing the 'snake'. 'You're really brave, Tracey,' he had said. 'I promise I'll never make fun of your name again.'

Tracey looked at the hedgehog. If Stanley should break his promise, it wouldn't hurt to have a spiky secret weapon up her sleeve (or in her schoolbag).

'Okay,' she told Hedgehogula. 'You can stay.'

'Of course I can,' said the hedgehog. 'Now tell me more about this strawberry milk . . .'

DEATH BY CLOWN

by

Tristan Bancks

'Hey, Tom.'

Oh no.

It's her.

On the phone.

Talking to me, Tom Weekly.

Why would she want to talk to me? I'm so nervous I want to throw up. This is the worst day of my life. I'm—

'Tom?'

'Yeah?'

Sasha. The cutest and smartest girl in Australia.

'Are you okay?' she asks.

What do you say to someone with eyes like blue sky, a voice like a mango smoothie and fresh, minty breath like an Arctic breeze? Not that I can smell it right now, but I can imagine it. So minty.

'Tom?'

She sounds a bit annoyed. I can't mess this up.

I always mess things up with Sasha. Like the time I told her I was attacked by a giant feral guinea pig, who bit off my toe. Why am I such a—

'We've got a spare front-row ticket to the circus tonight because my brother has to go to karate and Thalia and Leilani and Sophie and Brittany are busy. So do you want to come?'

Circus.

'Tom?'

'Huh?'

'I'm asking you to the circus.'

'Um . . .' I'm sweating. I try to tell myself that it's just because Sasha has called my house for the first time in our long on-again, off-again relationship. But I know that's not it.

'Mum's calling me,' Sasha says. 'I've got to get ready. Do you want to come or not, Tom?'

My head froths with fear and panic—white-faced, red-nosed, fuzzy-haired, polka-dotted panic. But this is Sasha, my kryptonite.

'Yes,' I whisper.

'"Yes" you'll come?'

'Yes,' I say again, slightly louder, my voice breaking in an awkward way.

'Great,' she says. Although she doesn't sound so

sure now. 'We'll pick you up in 15 minutes.'

'Fifteen,' I repeat.

'See you soon.' Sasha hangs up.

'I'm dead,' I say to the beeping phone line. I have front-row seats to my own death.

I press 'End' and place the phone on the kitchen bench. I have never admitted this to anyone other than my mother, but I have a morbid fear of clowns. And when I say 'morbid', I mean 'psychologically unhealthy'. And when I say 'psychologically unhealthy', I mean they freak me out. I can't be near them. But, in everyday life, that's fine. I just avoid little kids' birthday parties, certain fast food outlets . . . and circuses. I have my coulrophobia (fear of clowns) under control.

Or at least I thought I did. Until about 17 seconds ago.

Mum comes into the kitchen, takes a bag of baby peas from the freezer and pours them into boiling water on the stove. 'What's wrong?' she asks.

'Sasha,' I say.

'What about her?'

'She asked me out,' I say.

'Really! That's great. I think you're going to marry her one day.'

'No,' I say.

'You're not going to marry her?'

'No. Circus.'

'You're not going to marry her at the circus?'

'She asked me to go to the circus. In 15 minutes.'

'Oh dear,' she says. 'Did you say no?'

I shake my head.

'Well, it's probably about time you got over it. You were three years old, Tom.'

I think back to the painting that Mum did. She hung it on the wall over my bed on the night of my third birthday. It still smelt like oil paint. I don't think it ever really dried. The picture was of a tall, skinny clown in a blue polka-dot suit, red bow tie, fedora hat and evil eyes.

Every night from the age of three till I finally ripped the painting down when I was eight, he would slither out over the frame and into my bedroom. Some nights he would drop juggling balls onto my head for hours. Or strum an out-of-tune ukulele till four in the morning. Or sit right next to my ear and squeakily twist balloons into the shapes of werewolves, llamas and baboons.

I try to shake the clown from my thoughts, but there's no way out of this. Girls like Sasha don't just

call up every night and ask guys like me to go out with them. My pop always said, 'Never look a gift horse in the mouth.' I never knew what he meant. But maybe this is it—not that Sasha is a horse. Although she does have kind of a long face and she sometimes has sliced apples for morning tea.

What if I'd said no and she asked some other guy like Zane Smithers? They would start going out together. They would end up getting married and having three kids and a labradoodle and a house overlooking the ocean with secret passages and revolving bookcases. All because I'd said no to going to the circus.

Over my dead body will I let that happen.

Dead body.

Mine.

▲ ▲ ▲

The lights go down. Excitement swells—cheers and whistles and howls. Five hundred excited people are seated around the circus ring under the big top. Correction: 499 excited, one terrified.

'What do you really want to see?' Sasha asks, popping a piece of purple popcorn into her mouth.

'I love the tightrope and the hula hoops, but I can't wait for the clowns. They're so funny. My favourite clown is . . .'

I tune out. Even the mention of the word 'clown' dries out my tongue and dampens my armpits. I squinch my eyes closed. I should be happy. I'm sitting next to Sasha. I can smell her minty breath, hear her mango smoothie voice, and our knees even touched a few minutes ago.

Yet I am filled with dread. The clown from the painting over my bed slithers back into my mind. Wherever I would go in my bedroom his eyes would follow. Sometimes I'd feel him watching me in other rooms, too. And at school. Even on holidays at the beach. There's a phobia called anatidaephobia, which is the fear that—no matter where you are—a duck is watching you. Maybe that's what I have, except with clowns. No matter what I said, for years Mum wouldn't take the painting down. 'Don't be silly. Kids love clowns,' she would say. 'Don't you like my painting?'

BOOM!

There is an explosion and a burst of flame that sends shockwaves through the crowd. My heart leaps into my head. Ten trapeze artists swing down from the big top. Five let go and the other five catch them in midair. Water fountains erupt all around the ring. A long-haired motorbike stunt rider soars over a jump and comes to land in front of us. She skids to a stop on the sawdust floor, rips off her helmet and raises her hand for silence.

'Ladieeeees and gentlemennnnn! Welcome to Dingaling Brothers Circus, the most extraordinary display on Earth!'

'That's amazing,' Sasha says, squeezing my hand.

It is. For the next hour, we are dazzled by unbelievable magic, stunts and acrobatics. And you know what? Not a single clown. That is, until the lights go down after the human cannonball and I hear the honking sound of a cheap rubber horn. Every hair on my body stands to attention.

The lights snap on again. Not a slow fade but a violent snap.

A clown emerges from between the tall velvet curtains on the far side of the ring. He's driving a tiny, kid-sized fire truck, his knees up around his ears. He waves to the crowd and blows his horn over and over again. As he moves closer and closer, I start to realise who he is. He is not just any clown. His hair is black and he wears a blue polka-dot suit, a red bow tie and a fedora hat. He is the sweaty, demonic clown from my mother's painting.

I wet my pants. Not a lot, but definite leakage.

'I have to go to the toilet,' I tell Sasha, panicking. I stand and start to leave.

'Nooo, this is my favourite part. I love the clowns. Please stay.' She grabs my hand and pulls me back down. Clown-fear and Sasha-love battle to the death in my chest.

The crowd all around me is cracking up. As he zooms towards us I see that his truck has 'Giggles' written on the side. *Giggles the Clown*. He comes to a stop in front of us, his fire truck skidding in the sawdust. He falls out of the truck onto his face. The crowd erupts with laughter.

He stands, dusts himself off and looks directly at me.

He knows me.

He knows that I know that he knows me.

And he wants revenge for what I did to him.

Sweat stings my eyes. I slide down low in my chair.

Giggles motions to the crowd like he wants a helper. I slide down further in my seat, trying to become invisible. Giggles lowers his chin, glares at me through his thick brows, points and motions to me with one crooked, white-gloved finger.

Sasha claps wildly. 'Tom! It's you! He wants you!'

I can't get up.

'Just go!' Sasha says.

I shake my head, cross my arms, squinch my eyes shut again.

'Go on, young man!' says the grandma sitting to my right.

'How about you go, lady?' I snap.

'Get up, Tom!' says Sasha's dad. 'What's wrong with you?'

I shake my head. I have another flashback to the painting over my bed, the night he slipped out over the frame and tried to suffocate me with the world's unfunniest clown fart. It smelt like dead mice, ginger beer and cauliflower. I was drowning in it. I held my breath for almost two minutes before I could swim to the surface of that deathly stench. I wrestled him back into the picture frame and ripped the painting off the wall.

I dragged it outside in the dark of night and hid it in the shed behind the plastic tubs of camping gear and old tiles and tins of paint. Mum asked where the painting had gone, but I never, ever owned up to my crime. I thought that was the end of him, until tonight.

Someone yells, 'Boooo!' Someone else says, 'Come on, kid. Hurry up!'

When I still refuse to move, Sasha's dad jumps out of his seat, picks me up and puts me over his shoulder.

'No!' I struggle and pound my fists against his back to let me down, but he's too strong. He carries me into the ring. He dumps me on the ground next to Giggles, who takes me by the arm. Sasha's dad strides back to his seat to wild applause.

Giggles pulls something out of his pocket and holds it up to the crowd. He does not speak, just points and fake-smiles. It is a clown suit. From his other pocket he produces a bright orange wig. He turns to me with those bloodshot eyes of doom, oil paint dripping down his face. Spider webs and dead grass are tangled in the wig that pokes out from the edge of his fedora. He smells like our shed—lawnmower fuel and rat droppings. I want to run but he digs his long fingernails into the soft flesh of my upper arm. I look out at the crowd.

'Put it on!' they scream.

I look at Sasha. She's smiling at me with a face full of expectation. So I pull the stupid clown suit on.

It is white with rainbow spots and a pink-and-orange ruff around the neck. Giggles pulls the wig down hard on my head, then plants a kids' fire helmet on top. He slathers my face in white make-up using a paintbrush big enough to paint a house. He snaps a red nose on me and scrawls lipstick across my lips. The crowd loves every minute. He's a funny guy, Giggles.

He shoves me backwards into the small fire truck that he arrived in. My feet are hanging over the front because it's so small. There is a little steering wheel perched between my legs. Giggles holds up a large, silver, glittery box and pulls up an aerial. He flicks a switch and the fire truck takes off. Soon, the crowd is a blur. I am speeding around the ring with a demented clown at the controls. I am embarrassed and petrified, and hundreds of people are watching me. They start up a clap in time with the crazy circus music.

Giggles' sickly, black tongue squirms at the corner of his mouth as he stands in the centre of the ring, steering the truck with the remote. His eyes are narrow and he gleams with sweat. He throws an arm in the air and a thick wall of flame leaps from the floor right next to him.

Giggles turns the fire truck hard and it skids to a stop. I try to pull myself out of the truck, but it takes off again before I have a chance. I am heading directly towards the wall of fire. Surely this lunatic isn't going to drive a child through fire? There's no way I'll get through it without being toasted like a marshmallow.

The crowd seems to realise what is happening. They stop clapping as I speed towards the blaze.

My throat closes up. I'm only 20 metres from being burnt alive and I'm gaining speed. I can't jump out now—I'm going too fast. I grab the wheel and rip it to the right. The truck moves right but Giggles, with the remote control, steers me back towards the fire. I rip it to the left and Giggles steers me back again.

I can see the crowd behind him. They look worried, which worries me even more. People call out 'STOP!', but Giggles is hell-bent on killing me, I know it.

Tom Weekly does not go down without a fight. I decide to drive the truck right at him. I will face my fear and take him down. I've had enough. It's Tom Weekly vs Giggles the Clown, and the Gigmeister is going down.

He stands just to the left of the wall of fire. As I twist the wheel, charging towards him, I see a flicker of fear in his red-rimmed eyes. The speeding fire truck is ten metres from both the flames and the world's most dastardly clown. He steers me towards the fire, and I steer back. He steers me towards the fire again, and I steer back. I'm five metres away and I can feel the terrible inferno. Giggles is hunched over the remote control and is not about to give in. Good, because neither am I. I am two metres from the fire and there is a very real chance that I am about to be barbecued. Crowd members run into the ring towards us. Sasha's dad is one of them.

Now! I tear the wheel to the left and clamp it there with my hands and knees. I put every last shred of muscle and energy that I have into this.

The fire engine skids and feels like it's about to roll when the shiny silver bumper bar hits Giggles right in the shins. He screams, falls backwards, and his oversized clown shoes flip the truck up in an explosion of ladders and jingling bells. I am thrown out of the truck towards the devastating wall of fire. I hit the ground hard and flames lick my clown suit, setting my wig alight. My head is on fire, and I roll over and over to kill the flames. Someone from the crowd helps.

As soon as the flames are out, I look back. The truck has stopped dead, right on top of Giggles. His arms and legs are pinned beneath the vehicle. The remote control, aerial snapped, lies on the sawdust next to him.

Two clown paramedics run across the ring with a stretcher. Sasha and her dad reach me. I sit up.

Sasha gives me a huge hug. In that moment, feeling the warmth and kindness of her, and the relief of knowing that I am alive, my coulrophobia seems to slip away.

I am no longer afraid of clowns.

▲ ▲ ▲

Sasha holds my hand all the way home in the car.

'Goodnight, Tom,' she says when we pull up outside my house. She looks at me in a way she's never looked at me before. I gaze back.

'Alrighty then,' says her dad, switching on the car's interior light.

'Okay, g'night,' I say, climbing out of the car.

Sasha wipes the steam from the back window and watches me as they drive off. I float up my front path on an air-biscuit of Sasha-love. I knock on the front door. Footsteps. The door opens. Mum screams when she sees me dressed as a lightly toasted clown.

'What are you wearing *that* for?'

'Long story,' I say, pushing past her.

'How did you go with the clowns?'

'Good. I mean not good. I'll tell you in the morning,' I say, heading down the hall.

I shut the bathroom door and rest my back against it. I sniff the hand that Sasha was holding. I can smell her popcorny goodness. I decide to never wash that hand again. I figure I'll put it in a plastic bag when I shower.

I look at myself in the mirror. I have saved my life, overcome my fear of clowns and won the girl of my dreams—all in one night. I straighten my burnt, orange wig and adjust my nose. I look kind of cool. Sasha loves clowns. Maybe that's why she looked at me that way?

I smile at the mirror, then I bare my teeth like I'm about to eat a small child. Then I smile sweetly again. It's fun to be a clown. I squeeze the spurty flower stuck to my clown suit and water drips down the mirror, blurring my reflection.

I think back to Giggles being arrested and taken away in cuffs after receiving medical attention from the clown doctor. I guess Dingaling Brothers will probably be looking for someone to replace him. And for the first time in my life, I think I know what I want to be when I grow up.

A PERFECTLY NORMAL THURSDAY

by

Deborah Abela

It was a perfectly normal Thursday when there was a knock at the door of the Sneddley cottage.

'Are you expecting anyone?' Mrs Sneddley asked.

'Not that I am aware of,' Mr Sneddley answered.

Mr and Mrs Sneddley weren't the type of people who expected knocks on the door, mostly because they didn't have any friends. They once did, but that was a long time ago and the few relatives they had lived in a country far away where wild creatures with long tails hopped down the streets and may have gobbled them up.

Visitors were something that simply didn't happen.

Even strangers stayed away from their house, which sat crooked and grey beneath peeling paint. The plants were dead, there were prickles in the grass and the welcome mat had long since been taken to the tip.

There was another knock.

'There it is again,' Mr Sneddley said, not knowing what else to say.

There was a rather long pause before Mrs Sneddley said, 'I guess we better answer it.'

Mrs Sneddley turned the key and opened the door by the smallest of smidgeons.

And there she saw a parcel.

For many people, receiving a parcel would not cause the slightest fuss, because this is the kind of thing that happens with people and the places they live. There are knocks on doors followed by parcels arriving. The parcels are then opened to either surprise and delight or sometimes disappointment if they discover Grandma has sent underwear and socks for Christmas. Or maybe slices of ham if Grandma was a bit old and rickety.

It's all very normal.

Except if you're the Sneddleys.

They were never remembered by anyone who may send gifts. Or slices of ham.

But there was something else about this parcel that made it even more unusual.

It was attached to a young girl. Well, not *attached*, exactly, but held for dear life in her shivering hands.

'Can I help you?' Mrs Sneddley poked her nose through the opening.

The girl stood on their doorstep as if this was all perfectly normal. She wiped the melted snowflakes from her cheeks. 'Why, yes.' She was all smiles. 'I have a gift for you.'

This did nothing to clear things up for Mr Sneddley, who was standing behind his wife, leaning in as far as he could so he could hear every word.

'A gift for who?' Mrs Sneddley asked.

'If it's no bother, could I come inside? It's cold out here.' The girl was a bit soggy and the falling snow was making it worse.

Mrs Sneddley wasn't sure. She wasn't in the habit of letting strangers into her home and even though this one was small and harmless-looking, it was still something that she and Mr Sneddley just didn't do.

But the girl's cheeks were bright red, she wore no hat and there was a hole in the toe of her left boot.

'I suppose so.' Mrs Sneddley lifted the chain from its hook and opened the door wider.

The Sneddleys stepped back, partly from fear, but mostly from what could only be called 'a right stink'.

Mrs Sneddley held her nose and pointed at the little girl's boots, which seemed to be coated in manure. 'Better leave those outside.'

As she directed the girl to the fireplace, Mrs Sneddley's head swished wildly with thoughts of what she'd done.

Maybe the girl was a thief who'd come to steal their worldly possessions. Or she was a decoy for bigger thieves who were waiting in the bushes until the girl tricked her way inside with her cute ways and innocent eyes that fluttered with long curled lashes.

Maybe letting this girl inside would be the end of them.

The fire roared and crackled and the heat soaked right into the girl's bones, warming her fingers and especially those toes. She placed the parcel on the floor and rubbed her hands before the flames.

'That's very nice. Thank you.'

'You're welcome,' Mr Sneddley answered, still not sure why this perfectly normal Thursday had become so strange.

Even though the house looked quite run-down from the outside, inside was different. There were cabinets full of fine crockery that looked fit for a queen.

Mr Sneddley watched as the girl looked at their cabinets and thought perhaps that was why she was here. She was going to rob them so they had nothing left to call their own! His heart quickened. Oh why had they let her in?

Maybe he could shuffle her out the door before it was too late. He winced at the thought. He'd never rough-handled anyone, especially a child, but he was consoled by the idea that the snow would make a soft landing when he booted her out.

The girl sniffed. 'What's that smell?'

Mr Sneddley's thoughts of child-shuffling were interrupted.

'That's Mrs Sneddley's cake. We were about to have afternoon tea when we heard knocking.'

That was when she saw it. A small table set for two, and in the centre was a marvellous cake. It was covered in chocolate icing that dripped down the sides and was sprinkled with crescents of candied orange and curls of white chocolate.

The girl's stomach rumbled. It had been a long time since she'd eaten and the cake made her tremble so much that she worried she might collapse. 'It looks very delicious.'

'It is,' Mr Sneddley agreed. 'Mrs Sneddley makes

the finest cakes in the whole of Muddly Shire. She's won the Muddly Shire Cake Competition five times in a row. She's unbeatable.'

'Oh stop now,' Mrs Sneddley blushed.

'I won't,' Mr Sneddley said. 'Not when it's the truth.'

'Does that mean you're the best cake-maker in the world?'

Mr Sneddley stood taller. 'I reckon she'd have to be.'

'Now stop, both of you,' Mrs Sneddley said.

'People would come from miles around to our cake shop in town until . . . ' Mr Sneddley stopped, as if the words had been plucked from his mouth.

There was a small pause where no one knew what to say. Then Mrs Sneddley asked, 'Would you like some?'

The girl's stomach rumbled even more at the thought of eating. Using her best manners and her most polite voice she answered, 'Yes, please.'

After Mrs Sneddley sent her to the bathroom with a jumper, thick woollen tights and an extra large bar of soap, they sat down to tea. Mr Sneddley cut the cake, scooping up chocolatey slices and laying them carefully on each plate as if they were delicate pieces of art.

The girl tried to steady her hand as she lifted the fork. It took all her strength not to grab the cake and gobble it in one gulp. Instead, she slid the fork into the cake and placed a dainty sized portion in her mouth.

She closed her eyes. The cake made her feel light and dizzy. Her fingers and toes tingled. She worried that when she opened her eyes, she might actually be flying.

'It's truly the most delicious thing I have ever eaten.'

Mrs Sneddley smiled. 'It did turn out rather well.'

After another piece, the girl fell asleep in her chair. Just like that.

'What should we do?' Mrs Sneddley whispered.

All thoughts of shuffling the girl into the snow were gone from Mr Sneddley's mind. 'We'll put her to bed and in the morning she can be on her way.'

'The spare bed?' There was an inkling of fear in Mrs Sneddley's voice.

'It's time we put it to good use.' Mr Sneddley lifted the girl but as he did, she curled her arms around him and nuzzled into his neck. He wondered if this was a bad idea. If perhaps something had begun that was too late to stop.

Mrs Sneddley was thinking the same thoughts.

But what could they do?

Mr Sneddley carried the girl upstairs to a room filled with books and wooden toys and painted with bright sunflowers. He gently laid her down and Mrs Sneddley drew the covers to her chin. The girl snuffled a sleepy breath.

The Sneddleys stood above her. They felt light and dizzy. It had been a long time since they'd allowed visitors into their home and they hoped it was okay to break the rule this one time.

They tiptoed downstairs and it was only then they remembered the parcel. Mr Sneddley carefully opened it. Inside was a letter. It was crumpled and the words were faded and hard to read. It said:

For you to keep

It certainly was the most unusual Thursday they'd ever had.

▲ ▲ ▲

The girl slept for two days and when she woke she was famished. Over a breakfast of porridge and honey and hot buttery raisin toast, Mr Sneddley asked. 'What's your name?'

'Skylar.'

'Where do you belong, Skylar?'

She shrugged. 'Nowhere.'

'Everyone belongs somewhere,' Mrs Sneddley said.

'Not me. When I was a baby, I was dumped on the doorstep of two people who smelled like cabbage and, when I was older, made me clean the house and scrape cow manure off their boots. We lived on a dairy farm. There was a lot of cow manure.'

'They'll be missing you,' Mrs Sneddley said.

'They'll be missing their clean boots, that's all.'

'Surely not.'

'They said I had a dangerous imagination and the only thing for it was to send me to bed without supper. Which happened a lot.'

'Maybe they meant well,' Mrs Sneddley said, even though it was hard to imagine how they could.

'You'll miss school,' Mr Sneddley said.

'I've never been.'

An unexpected anger rose in Mr Sneddley's chest.

Mrs Sneddley asked, 'So how did you write the letter?'

'I didn't. It was in the box with me when I was found on the doorstep. I was given a home the first time, so I thought it might work again.'

'Still,' Mrs Sneddley decided. 'We should take you back.'

But they didn't.

One day became another, and Skylar stayed. Mrs Sneddley showed her how to find the plumpest berries in the forest and Mr Sneddley taught her to read and write. 'Not reading is like not eating,' he said. 'A child needs both or they simply waste away.'

Every night, he read to her in bed. 'We'll start with *Charlotte's Web*, one of our favourites.'

Skylar loved the story of the little girl called Fern and how she saved the runt pig called Wilbur. Mr Sneddley put on a different voice for every character, so it felt as if they were real.

One night, after Mr Sneddley finished another chapter, Skylar asked, 'Why do you have a children's bedroom?'

Mr Sneddley took a long time to answer. 'We once had a little boy, but his lungs were weak and he didn't last.'

'Is that why you don't have a cake shop any more?'

Mr Sneddley gave a single, sad nod.

Skylar reached out and took his hand and all thoughts of her leaving were gone.

▲ ▲ ▲

It was during a walk in the woods gathering berries for another of Mrs Sneddley's cakes that Skylar heard a rustling in the trees. She froze, worried that it was a bear or a wolf, or a forest monster with pointed fangs, when a small dog emerged.

'Hey, little fella.' Skylar tickled him under the chin. 'What are you doing out here?'

The dog barked and ran back into the forest, before stopping and barking again, as if he wanted her to follow.

The Sneddleys told Skylar not to wander too far into the forest because it was easy to get lost, but the barking became more insistent. She followed him through the trees, until she came upon a woman sitting on the ground, with mud splattered on her dress and hands.

'Are you okay?'

'Yes, perfectly fine, apart from slipping in the jolly mud.' The woman patted the dog. 'You're a loyal boy, Bertie.'

Skylar thought she recognised the woman. 'Do I know you?'

'Perhaps, but I don't believe we have met officially. I'm Queen Elizabeth.'

Skylar scowled. 'I'm sorry?'

'We have a home not far from here and I was taking one of my afternoon strolls. It clears the head for all that royal business one has to do.'

‘So you really are the Queen?’

‘Yes, don’t you believe me?’

‘It’s just that . . . ’ Skylar squinted at the woman’s muddy boots and scarf tied around her unruly grey curls. ‘You don’t look very queenly.’

‘No, I suspect not,’ she said. ‘But you don’t have to look like a queen to be one. It’s how you are inside.’

‘How you are *inside*?’

‘Yes, that and other things like how you treat people and not losing your temper when someone takes the last jam tart. Even though that is annoying. Oh, and how you hold a cup of tea.’ She demonstrated by holding out a pinkie. ‘Speaking of tea, do you know where one may acquire a cup?’

‘I know where you can get tea *and* the best cake in the world.’

‘Really? Oh, I do love cake. My royal doctor says I shouldn’t, but his rules give me a pain in my royal behind.’

Skylar giggled as she helped the Queen to her feet and led the way through the forest to the Sneddley cottage.

Where she knocked on the door.

Inside, Mr and Mrs Sneddley looked up.

‘Are you expecting anyone?’ Mrs Sneddley asked.

'Not that I am aware of,' Mr Sneddley answered.

There was a small pause before Mrs Sneddley said, 'I guess we better answer it.'

When she opened the door, her mouth gaped open.

'This is Queen Elizabeth,' Skylar said. 'I've invited her over for tea and cake.'

'I . . . I . . . ' Mrs Sneddley stopped, unable to say more. Her face was pale and her mouth was still wide open. Mr Sneddley stood behind her looking very much the same.

Skylar worried they weren't well and was about to ask if they felt okay.

When Mrs Sneddley slammed the door.

'I'm sorry,' Skylar apologised. 'They're not used to visitors.'

She knocked again.

Urgent whispers were heard from inside.

This time, Mr Sneddley opened the door and stared at the Queen who stood in the doorway in a way that no queen had ever done before. 'Our humblest apologies,' he said, bowing so low Skylar worried he'd topple over, 'Your Majesty.'

'Not a bother,' said the Queen. 'It can be discombobulating to meet a queen. Even though one has never had a door slammed in one's face before. But now I would very much like some cake if that is possible.'

'Of course.'

Mrs Sneddley prepared the tea while Skylar set the table and Bertie curled up in front of the fire. Mr Sneddley cut the cake. It was a honey cake with swirls of lavender icing and decorated with Skylar's freshly picked berries.

The Queen held her fork in the air. She was quite hungry after her walk and it took all her strength not to grab the cake and gobble it in one gulp. Instead, she slid the fork carefully into the cake and placed a dainty sized portion in her mouth.

The Sneddleys and Skylar watched as the Queen closed her eyes and smiled.

'Do you feel light and dizzy?' Skylar asked.

'Yes!' the Queen said. 'And my fingers and toes are tingling.'

'That's because Mrs Sneddley is the best cake-maker in the world.'

'She's won the Muddly Shire Cake Competition five times in a row,' Mr Sneddley said. 'She's unbeatable.'

'Oh stop now,' Mrs Sneddley blushed.

'I won't,' Mr Sneddley said. 'Not when it's the truth.'

'Well I think . . . ' the Queen began when a giant burp escaped from her mouth. 'Oh dear,' she said. 'I'm terribly sorry for my extraordinarily bad royal manners.'

Skylar giggled, and so did the Queen and the Sneddleys.

'That's perfectly fine, Your Highness,' Mr Sneddley said. 'It is an honour to be in the presence of a royal burp.'

Which made them all giggle even more.

The Queen regaled the Sneddleys and Skylar with stories of royal mishaps, especially with Bertie, who it turned out could be quite cheeky, until the sun had almost fallen behind the horizon.

'My royal staff will be wondering where I am. Thank you for the most delicious afternoon.' She shook Mr and Mrs Sneddley's hands and walked back into the forest.

'Well how about that?' said Mr Sneddley. He was still finding it hard to believe they'd had tea and cake with the Queen. 'The Queen!'

'It really was quite something,' Mrs Sneddley said.

It was the second visitor they'd had in years and, despite what Mr and Mrs Sneddley thought of visitors, it wasn't so bad after all.

It was even rather nice.

▲ ▲ ▲

Winter passed and Skylar grew taller, her cheeks grew rosier and she was reading books on her own. Smaller ones at first, but she had to start somewhere, Mr Sneddley said.

Then, one day, there was another knock on the door.

'Are you expecting anyone?' Mrs Sneddley asked.

'Not that I am aware of,' Mr Sneddley answered.

'I guess we'd better answer it.' Mrs Sneddley swung the door open.

She gasped at the sight of a small group of people.

Led by the Queen.

'I hope you don't mind,' the Queen said, 'but this is Marge, Vera and Thelma from my book club.'

The Queen held up her book.

'*Charlotte's Web*!' Skylar cried. 'That's my favourite.'

'Ours too! But before we started our club, I was telling them about Mrs Sneddley's cake and they wondered if they could try some too.'

'If that's okay,' Marge said.

'We won't stay long,' Vera added.

'We promise,' Thelma promised.

'Of course,' Mrs Sneddley said, wondering where she might put them all. 'Please come in.'

Mrs Sneddley prepared the tea while Skylar set the table and Mr Sneddley found some boxes and laid a plank across them with cushions so everyone fitted snugly around the table.

Mr Sneddley cut the cake, carefully handing out each slice.

'Deeee-licious,' Marge said.

'Scrumptious,' Vera added.

'Sensational,' Thelma sighed.

'I told you so.' the Queen smiled. 'Skylar, so why is *Charlotte's Web* your favourite book?'

Skylar paused. There were so many reasons, but there was one that stood above all the others.

'I didn't know living in the country was about more than wiping cow poo off boots.'

The Queen's laugh lifted into the ceiling. 'I couldn't have said it better myself.'

And so the Queen and her friends and the Sneddleys and Skylar ate cake and talked about books until Skylar couldn't stay awake any longer. Mr Sneddley carried her upstairs, tucked her into bed and quietly tiptoed from the room, when Skylar noticed her parcel caught in the glow of her nightlight.

She crept out of bed and held the letter and, for the very first time, she read out loud, 'For you to keep.'

Skylar smiled. She carefully folded the note and placed it into the box, which she slipped beneath her bed, and fell asleep to the sound of voices and laughter that rose from below.

SIR BUM

by

Tony Wilson

My name is Harland Baum. Mum tells me she and Dad thought twice about calling me Harland because they thought kids might tease me. 'But it's a grand name,' she says. 'It's a name fit for a president or prime minister.'

They should have thought three times. They should have run it through the primary school playground filter.

What's short for Harland?

Harry.

Now say it three times.

Harry Baum. Harry Baum. Hairy Bum.

Ha! Did you just say 'Hairy Bum'?

Haaaaaa! Hairy Bum! Get it? His name is Hairy Bum!

My backside is not hairy, by the way. It's a rear end of standard ten-year-old non-hairiness. But the playground doesn't care. It doesn't help that my bum is bigger and rounder than it might ideally be once your nickname is 'Hairy Bum'. Overall, I'm a big and round kid. Mum says that if anyone ever calls me fat, I should tell a teacher straight away. But they don't. Not even the mean kids.

Everyone's plenty happy just calling me Hairy Bum.

▲ ▲ ▲

The Backwash Twins aren't so much mean as borderline insane. Our teacher, Ms Keenan-Mount, says they're 'vigorous'. I say they're crazy.

They're not really named Backwash, either, any more than I'm Hairy Bum. Their real names are Mickey and Maurice Backhouse. Unlike me—they invented their own nickname in Year Three, when they spent two whole terms stealing drink bottles and deliberately backwashing into the nozzles.

'Enjoy!' they'd guffaw, as they handed the drink bottle back. 'Ha! There's a little present in there from the Backwash Twins.'

None of us can tell the Backwash Twins apart. They both have shaggy blond hair, tanned skin and giant overlapping front teeth. They both wear baggy shorts, basketball singlets, and backwards-facing baseball caps. They both have disgustingly similar backwashing techniques, which involve plenty of back-of-throat work. Eventually, Scarlett Tremayne's mum complained to the school. The Backwash Twins terrorised our drinking equipment no more.

The Backwash Twins would be easier to avoid if they didn't live two doors up from me. I often see them climbing onto their roof and then leaping with blood-curdling screams onto a trampoline below. Once I even saw a Backwash Twin on old Mrs Branchflower's roof, the one between our house and theirs. He was just perched up there, throwing rocks. I wondered if they'd one day invade our roof, those insane tile-hopping Backwashes.

They sometimes knock on the door to ask me over to play. 'Yo, Mrs Bum! Can the great Harland Bum come over?'

Mum always says tightly that 'the name is Baum, rhymes with storm' and that I'm busy with piano practice. Normally I hate piano, but anything to make good Mum's excuse. Anything to avoid play-dates skipping daintily across neighbourhood rooftops with the Backwashes.

▲ ▲ ▲

On the day it all happened, there was a knock at the front door after school.

Mum answered. 'Well, hello there.' I could tell by the warm note of surprise that she liked the look of whoever it was.

'Hello, Mrs Baum,' said a young girl's voice, doing a bang-up job of rhyming with storm. 'Is Harland there?'

I peered around my mum's ample behind to see who it was.

Far out! It was Louisa Lim! Louisa Lim is the funniest, feistiest, sportiest, brainiest, everything-iest girl in Year Five. She has thick, wild, black hair, which she never ties back, even when she does high jump, which actually cost her first place in the school sports carnival last term. She has long limbs and perfect skin, which shows off teeth so straight and so white that I find myself just staring at them whenever Queen Louisa deigns to speak to me—which is normally about once or twice a year.

So what was Louisa Lim doing on my doorstep?

'Would Harry like to come out for a play?' She smiled. Those teeth were working their magic on Mum now. 'Of course,' Mum replied. 'I mean, I'd have to ask him, but . . . look, he's right here and as you can see, he's not busy . . . '

Five minutes later Louisa and I were walking

down the steps of our porch.

'Hi,' Louisa said, arching one of her perfect eyebrows.

'Hi,' I said, feeling very confused.

'Hi!' the Backwash Twins yelled, jumping out from behind the two cumquat bushes that frame our driveway.

I nearly had a heart attack. Louisa laughed, and slapped me on the back. 'I hope you don't mind,' she said. 'Mikey and Maurice do martial arts with me after school on Thursdays. My mum picks me up from their house. They said you wouldn't come out unless I did the knocking.'

'Yeeehaaaa!' hollered one of the Backwashes, and jumped onto my back to ride me like a cowboy. While I staggered, the other Backwash jumped on him to wrestle him to the nature strip. They only stopped when Louisa pointed out a dog turd they were about to roll in.

No, not vigorous, Ms Keenan-Mount. Crazy.

▲ ▲ ▲

'We've invented a game called "One Two Three Bum",' said one of the Backwash Twins as he performed some impossible twisting somersault combination on the trampoline. It was one of those super bouncy, in-ground, Olympic-sized numbers. 'You gotta get on here! We all gotta hold hands!'

Louisa grabbed me by the hand. I was so surprised I forgot to object to what would no doubt be some insane and possibly deadly Backwash Twins® production.

Mikey Backwash started to explain the rules. I found out it was Mikey because Louisa said, 'Cool, Mikey!' after he finished. I wasn't really listening to the rules because I was still thinking about *Louisa Lim holding my hand*.

Maurice, the other Backwash Twin, said, 'And then we go, "One Two Three BUM!" and do a "sit" together.'

We started bouncing. We started bouncing high —much higher than I felt comfortable bouncing. I could see over the Backhouses' fence into the nature reserve that bordered our back fence too. I could see old Mrs Branchflower watering her dahlias next door. All four of us hit the trampoline mat at exactly the same time. I was still holding hands with Louisa. Louisa's hand was about five thousand times less clammy than Maurice's. We were getting serious elevation now. Maurice and Louisa were such good bouncers they were almost pulling me up with them.

'One Two Three BUM!' we shouted, and we all did a sit.

My trampoline skills are not world class, but I can do a sit.

We let go of each other's hands and landed in perfect synch. It actually felt quite glorious. I laughed along with Louisa and the Backwashes. Maybe I'd been wrong all along? Maybe stupid, reckless games where you could possibly kill yourself are fun and worth playing? Did I want to play again? Yeah! I reached for Louisa's lovely slender hand . . .

. . . only for a Backwash Twin to grab my hand first!

'Can I have this dance?' he giggled maniacally. I'd forgotten which twin was which again. The other Backwash Twin grabbed my other hand. They really were completely identical, right down to hand clamminess. Louisa was now opposite, staring at me with her beautiful eyes. We made our circle.

'Okay, Bum, we sit on "Bum",' said the Backwash Twin to my right.

'Yeah, on "Bum", Hairy Bum!' giggled the Backwash Twin to my left.

We found our rhythm. I might have been unsteady but the Backwash Twins kept me in perfect time. Louisa was as graceful at trampolining as she is at everything else.

Bounce, bounce, bounce.

We were getting higher now.

Bounce, bounce, bounce.

The weight of the four of us almost made the mat sag to the ground.

Bounce, bounce, bounce.

The leaves of the overhanging lilly pilly brushed against my head.

'One!'

Oh dear, this feels a bit high.

'Two!'

The springs screamed as they flung us skywards.

'Three!'

Get through this. Just close your eyes and get through this!

On either side, I felt a tug as Mikey and Maurice pulled on my arms. However high those two were, they were throwing *me* that little bit higher.

They let go.

I flapped my arms.

I was wildly out of control.

I attempted a sit.

I landed that fraction of a second after the three of them.

'BUUUUUM!!'

It wasn't double-bouncing. That's for when there are two people on the trampoline. It wasn't triple-bouncing either, which happens with groups of three. This was quadruple-bouncing, which I don't think even had a name before this moment.

I was flung from the mat like a human cannon-ball. If my trajectory had been straight, I would have disappeared into the topmost branches of the lilly pilly above, before making a safe, if terrifying, fall back to earth. But my sit had not been good. The throw from the Backwash Twins had tossed me off balance, and I'd hit the mat at an awkward angle.

When I opened my eyes, I was flying.

Away from the trampoline.

Away from the Backhouses' house.

Away and across and over their back fence.

I heard Louisa scream with terror. The high-pitched giggles of the Backwashes died as they realised the seriousness of what was happening. The wind whooshed in my ears. I experienced the sensation of defying gravity for as long as a trampoline-powered human has ever defied gravity. I must have flown ten, maybe even 20 metres. The ground had to be coming. I cried out, and prepared myself for the pain.

Then somebody else cried out. It was a short, guttural shout, mixed with a swear word, made by a man in the nature reserve. I saw him at the very last second, just after he sighted me. He was wearing a black beanie, and had big, wide bloodshot eyes. There was no way I was going to miss him.

Whoooooomph!

My legs scissored either side of his head, and my famously ample backside smashed into his shoulders.

Louisa told me later that the landing was graceful. That I looked like an oversized jockey falling from the sky to straddle a collapsing horse.

'Sorry,' I said to the man in the beanie who had broken my fall.

The man said nothing. Was he dead? I was relieved to feel his chest moving. I was still sitting on his head with my bum.

'I'll get off you now,' I said.

No reply. The man was out cold.

I started to get up, amazed that not a single part of me was injured.

Then I heard the sirens.

Then I saw a sprinting SWAT team, all in Kevlar vests, guns drawn.

Then I saw the man's gun in the grass, gleaming in the twilight, just out of reach.

'Get away from that man!' one of the police yelled.

'He's armed and dangerous!'

I stood bolt upright. I placed my hands in the air, as if I was the one in trouble. Three police sprinted over to the unconscious man and snapped cuffs on him. A policewoman flung her body in front of mine, as if acting as a human shield.

The man didn't move. He was still knocked out.

The police finally began to relax.

We all stared at the man in the beanie lying unconscious on the ground.

One of the cops looked at me. 'How the heck did you do that, kid?'

▲ ▲ ▲

He was a very bad man. I won't go into details about how bad. All I will say is that he'd already fired his gun that afternoon, and he planned on firing it again.

I was hailed as a hero. The police took me back to the station to take a statement. It was weird watching them type out the rules to 'One Two Three Bum'. The officer in charge told me that the Backhouse twins had said the game was called 'One Two Three Sit'. I corrected the record. I said it was definitely 'One Two Three Bum', and that Maurice and Mikey had invented the game. The police typed everything up. I hoped the Backwash Twins wouldn't go to gaol for lying in their statement.

The story of my flight was front page in the newspaper the next day. The headline said 'CANNON-BOY HERO'. Louisa was interviewed for the article. 'He steered his way through the air so he could disarm the man,' Louisa said. 'Harry had no thoughts for his own safety.'

Mum read the story out loud the next morning over tea and marmalade. She actually started crying when she read the last line: 'He may only be ten years old, but today Harland Baum is the toast of the nation.'

'Harland Baum,' Mum sniffed, as she showed Dad the page. 'What did I tell you? A name fit for a prime minister or a president!'

Dad ruffled my hair. 'They won't be calling you Hairy Bum today, kiddo.'

▲ ▲ ▲

They didn't call me Hairy Bum.

They called me Cannon-boy, Cannon-Baum, Baum-trooper, the Bumminator, Bumbo the Bumaphant, Flight of the Bummingbird, The Fall Guy, Bumpty Dumpty, and Hairy Poodini. And those are only the names the Backwash Twins thought up.

I didn't mind. Those two were almost as excited as I was to have been involved in some backyard trampolining, crime-fighting heroics.

'Really, I don't know why you're gettin' all the credit,' one Backwash Twin said. 'It was me who kinda aimed you at that dude.'

'No, it was me!' yelled the other Backwash, and he jumped onto his brother's back. They wrestled in true Backwash style, and it only ended when Maurice rolled in a melted ice-cream.

I knew it was Maurice because Louisa said, 'Stand up, Maurice, you've rolled in a melted ice cream.'

She also turned to me and said, 'You were the

actual hero, Harry,' and gave me a pat on the shoulder.

Principal Wheeler said something similar in front of the whole school. We were at Thursday assembly in the gym. Principal Wheeler asked the Backwashes, Louisa and me to stand up. Then she introduced a politician whose name was the Honourable George Gargle. Mr Gargle said some things about civic duty. He then said some things about true courage. He then told a story about his childhood that was very long and very boring, and he kind of lost the audience. Then Mr Gargle said, 'These four brave children will be honoured next week by the Governor. They will come to Government House to receive a Medal of Honour and a Royal Certificate.'

The Backwash Twins began doing serious high fives.

Principal Wheeler said, 'That's enough, boys. Mr Garville might not award those Royal Certificates if you're not careful.'

That's when I worked out that he was called Garville, not Gargle.

We sat back down. One of the Backwashes gave me a hug and a kiss on the cheek. The other one danced in his seat and started singing a little song, 'We're getting a cert-if-i-cate! We're getting a cert-if-i-cate!'

'You can call me Dame Louisa,' Louisa whispered, and gave me a high five with that lovely and not at all clammy palm.

'You can call me Sir Backwash,' said one of the twins.

'No, I want to be Sir Backwash,' said the other.

'You can be *Lord* Backwash!' the first one replied. They started to wrestle, just as Principal Wheeler was awarding the Golden Lunchbox for the class that produces the least rubbish.

The politician formerly known as Gargle stared at the twins. He might have been having second thoughts about inviting the Backwashes to Government House.

'And I guess I can be Sir Bum,' I said quietly, and mainly to Louisa.

'Sir Bum!' the Backwashes repeated, not quietly. 'That's fantastic! You *absolutely must* be Sir Hairy Bum!'

Assembly was over. The procession music started to play. The Backwash Twins dragged me to my feet and heaved me up onto their shoulders.

'Arise for Sir Bum!' one of the Backwash Twins declared to the gymnasium.

'All hail Sir Bum!' the other one shouted.

I offered a tentative wave, a bit like the Queen. Hundreds of kids rose to their feet and cheered.

'Sir Bum! Sir Bum! Sir Bum!'

That's how we exited. Principal Wheeler and the politician smiling wryly at the head. Followed by Lady Louisa. Then me, chaired by the Backwash Twins, feeling happy and heroic.

'Sir Bum!' the whole school chanted as we made our way. 'Hooray for Sir Bum!'

I waved and acted dignified. All the way out into the sunshine.

▲ ▲ ▲

My name is Harland Baum, although my friends call me 'Sir Bum'.

NUTBUSH

by

Meredith Costain

I dangle the cat treat above Flossy's tiny nose.

'Flossy,' I say. 'Sit.'

Flossy gives me the stink eye.

'Come on, Flossy,' I beg. 'You *love* cat treats.'

Flossy doesn't move. She hasn't moved the last ten times I asked her to sit, either.

'You're doing it all wrong,' Dev says, grabbing the treat out of my hand.

'Sit,' he says, his voice all deep and commanding.

Flossy looks bored.

Jasmine sighs. 'You two obviously know nothing. Cats are really smart. They're not going to do something a dumb dog would do.'

'So what *can* they do?' I ask. 'Play handball? Take a specky? Make me a chocolate milkshake?'

I'm getting a bit desperate. Make that a lot desperate. There are only two weeks to go till the Best-trained Dog Competition. The competition that Boof Finkle wins every year with his dog Crusher.

Boof is in Year Six and thinks he rules the school. Just for once, *I* want to be up on that stage, accepting the Golden Dog Biscuit trophy from our principal, Mrs Martini.

There's only one teensy tiny problem. I don't have a dog.

But I'm really hungry for that Dog Biscuit. So I've decided to enter Flossy instead. In disguise, of course. My baby sister has this really fluffy poodle onesie that fits Flossy perfectly. All I have to do is zip her into it on the day—Flossy, not my little sister—and show the judges what a well-trained cat . . . er, dog . . . she is.

Jasmine taps my arm. 'What about a high five?'

I stare at her. 'What. Now? I haven't even won yet.'

Jasmine rolls her eyes. 'I meant Flossy, Sam. You could train Flossy to do a high five.'

'Oh. Right,' I say, scratching my head. 'Sounds . . . great.'

I'm just about to give up on the whole idea when a butterfly flits past my nose and lands on a flowery branch just past my head. Quicker than you can say ‘winners are grinners’, Flossy’s up on her hind legs, batting at it with her paw.

And then I have a brilliant idea. Flossy’s always up on her hind legs. Trying to swipe snacks off the kitchen bench. Fiddling with the pencils on my desk. Staring out the window. It’s like she thinks she’s one of those meerkats you see at the zoo. I could pretend I’ve trained her to stand up tall like that and beg, like you see on those ads on TV for fancy cat food.

I’m all excited now. I grab another treat out of the box and hold it up high above Flossy’s head. Sure enough, she rises up . . . and up . . . and up . . . and swipes at the treat.

Only she misses, and gets my arm instead. (Did I mention that Flossy has very sharp claws? I’m actually thinking of changing her name to Slasher. Or Ripper. Or Razor. Or maybe a combination of all three.)

‘Oww,’ I say. And also, ‘Eww.’ There’s blood. I hate blood. Especially when it’s mine.

Flossy scoots up the front of our fence and over the top into Mrs Pumphrey’s garden. Flossy loves Mrs Pumphrey. She’s always going over there.

She settles down on a chair on her front verandah

and gives me another stink eye. Then she lifts one leg and licks at a spot under her tail.

We stand there in silence, thinking about how Flossy has robbed me of the chance to finally win the Golden Dog Biscuit.

Then Jasmine points out a sad pile of fluff a bit further along the verandah.

'What about her?' she asks.

'Zippy?' I say. Zippy is Mrs Pumphrey's dog. She's about 90 years old. And trust me, she grew out of her name a long time ago.

Jasmine nods. 'Zippy!' she calls. 'Here, Zippy!'

Zippy thumps her tail on the verandah boards a few times, then collapses from the effort.

Jasmine waves a cat treat at her. 'Come to Jazzy.'

I stare at Jasmine. 'You're not thinking what I think you're thinking, are you?'

'Sure,' says Jasmine. 'Why not?'

Dev blinks at us blankly.

'Haven't you ever heard that saying, "You can't teach an old dog new tricks?" Anyway, she can't see you. She's blind as.'

'Well, at least she's an actual dog,' Jasmine snorts. 'Not a giant, razor-clawed cat dressed up in a poodle onesie.'

She's right. As usual.

'Flossy!' I call. 'Come. Here. *Now!*'

Flossy arches her back—then yawns.

'Here, kitty, kitty.' I rattle the treat box. 'Look. I've got treats.'

Flossy lifts a leg and starts licking her bottom again.

'Right. That's it,' I warn her. 'No more treats for YOU.'

Flossy jumps down lightly from her comfy chair and pads around to the back of Mrs Pumphrey's house, like it's her new home. And we all troop back inside, defeated.

▲ ▲ ▲

Dev and Jasmine and I are hanging outside the local milk bar on our bikes. And then guess who else turns up?

Boof Finkle and his prize-winning dog, Crusher.

'What's this?' he says. 'A meeting of the Losers' Club?'

'It is now,' Jasmine fires back. Go, Jaz!

Boof's eyes narrow, just for a second.

'I taught Crusher a new trick this morning,' he tells us. 'Wanna see?'

'Sure,' I say.

Boof tells Crusher to sit.

'Is that it?' I snigger. Then instantly regret it.

'I taught him how to pee on command,' Boof says. 'On bikes.' Then he grins. 'Which bike would you like him to pee on first?'

Nobody moves. Not even an eyelid.

Boof looks around, then points to Dev's shiny new BMX Pro Majestic. He loves that bike. It's taken him a whole year of car-washing to save up for it. 'This one?'

Crusher turns his head towards the bike, his piggy eyes bulging. His whole body is quivering.

'B-but I don't want my bike peed on,' Dev stammers, looking to us for help. 'My mum will kill me if I come home with a stinky bike.'

'Tough,' says Boof.

He holds up his left hand, his middle finger pointing skyward. 'Crusher?'

Crusher cocks his leg, ready for action.

'Pee!' thunders Boof.

A warm stream of dog pee cascades over the Majestic's frame, then trickles down from the custom-made pedals to the pavement.

'Now give Sammy boy a kiss,' Boof tells his dog.

'Nooooooo!' I scream as Crusher lunges at me. 'Keep him off me!'

But it's no good. Crusher has me pinned firmly to the ground, right next to the pool of pee. He's licking my face all over with his stinky, germy tongue.

Boof gives a low whistle and Crusher springs back to his side.

'See you all on Monday,' Boof tells Jasmine. Then he and Crusher lope off into the distance.

Crusher's doggy dribble is making me gag. Dev passes me one of his used tissues.

'Eww,' I say, when I see the snot on it. I wipe my face then hand it back.

'Gross,' he says, when he sees the dog drool. Then he puts it back into his pocket.

I have to admit, Boof's actually pretty good at training dogs. Winning that competition is going to be trickier than I thought.

Especially as I still don't have a dog.

▲ ▲ ▲

Ten minutes later we're back on our bikes (after giving Dev's a good going-over with the milk bar hose) and pedalling off down Main Street. We hang a left onto one of the dirt tracks that runs off it, straight into bushland.

We're just riding past some ghost gums when Dev suddenly hits the brakes on the Majestic, and I crash into him.

Jasmine stops to help me up.

'What did you do that for?' I say to Dev, rubbing my knee.

'Listen!' Dev snaps, obviously spooked.

'To what?'

'That howling sound. Can't you hear it?'

'Nope.' I look at Jasmine. 'Can you?'

Jasmine wrinkles her nose. 'We-ell . . . Maybe a bit.'

And then I hear it too. My good knee starts shaking like a pair of maracas in the school band. Not that I'd ever let on.

'What do you reckon it is?' Dev asks.

I swivel my head from side to side. 'Could be aliens. Old Joe Rossi reckons he saw a spaceship land out here a few months back.'

'Seriously?' Dev says, his face pale.

I wave my hands around, alien-style. '*Oo ee oo ee!*'

'Sssshh,' Jasmine snaps. 'Listen!'

We listen. We can still hear the howling. But now there's a new sound as well.

Jasmine climbs back onto her bike. 'It's dogs.' She tilts her chin to the left. 'And it's coming from over that way.'

My ears prick up. Dogs?! I'm there.

▲ ▲ ▲

We keep riding until we run into a fence, covered with handpainted signs.

'This must be Old Ma Greevy's place,' I say.

'How did you know that?' asks Dev, impressed.

'It's written on the letterbox.'

I prop my bike against the fence, checking out the gate. It's big. And covered with rusty padlocks and strips of barbed wire.

I rattle it. Locked tight.

The howls and barks grow louder.

'Looks like we'll have to go over the top,' I say.

'B-b-but we can't go in there,' Dev stammers.

'Why not?' asks Jasmine.

'Old Ma Greevy. I've heard she's a witch. And she's got a cupboard full of pointy things. She'll skin us alive. And then eat us for breakfast.'

I've heard those stories too. Then I remember something else. Something important. 'Danny Vella went missing somewhere around here last summer.'

Jasmine sighs. 'His family moved up north for his dad's work, der brain.'

Phew. No problems then. I throw back my shoulders and take a commanding step forward. 'Team? We're going in.'

▲ ▲ ▲

We're over the top and slinking stealthily towards a creepy-looking old house at the back of the property. Think MAXIMUM creepy. Old vines curling around the verandah posts. Faded paint flaking off ancient wooden shutters. A weathervane with a grinning goblin on top moving slowly back and forth.

Creak . . . Creak . . .

The dogs are going off big time. They must be able to hear us coming.

And if the dogs can hear us . . .

Dev's rattling on about something again.

'Sssssshhhhh,' I tell him. 'Keep your voice down.'

'Smemeevyemwmrboilmmwmoil,' he whispers.

'Huh?' Jasmine says.

'I also heard Old Ma Greevy boils kids in oil,' he shouts. Then claps a hand over his mouth.

'And how exactly is she going to do that?' asks Jasmine.

'In . . . th-there,' says Dev, pointing to a rusty tank attached to the side of the house. There are some old drums stacked next to it. *Oil* drums. My knee starts shaking again. I've heard that story too.

'That's a *water* tank,' Jasmine sighs. 'For collecting rain water? From the roof?'

'So?' I say. Smarty pants. How come she has to know *everything*? 'It's obviously for cooling down the kids once they've been boiled in oil. So she can eat them straightaway.'

'Yeah,' Dev agrees. 'Good point.'

Jasmine glares at us. 'Look. Do you want to find out what's going down here or not?'

'Umm . . . Maybe tomorrow?' Dev offers.

'Let's do it now,' I say. I take a deep breath, then follow Jaz over to a side window.

We bob down and peek through it. Inside, there are dogs. A *lot* of dogs. Just milling around.

A little white dog with a cheeky grin is balancing on top of a narrow ledge. Then he suddenly does this ginormous leap, twisting his body as he soars through the air, and lands on top of a sideboard on the other side of the room. And he doesn't even smash anything! He's like a circus dog!

'How did all these dogs even get here?' Dev asks.

'Are there any stories about Old Ma Greevy having lots of dogs?' I ask him.

He shakes his head. 'Nope. Just the witchy ones. And the oil boiling.'

'Where is she, anyway?' Jasmine asks. 'You'd think she'd have come outside to see what set them all off.'

'Maybe the dogs have been kidnapped by evil dog thieves,' I say. 'You know, like in that movie with all the spotty dogs? *101 Dalmatians*? And they need us to rescue them.'

'And maybe the evil dog thieves have kidnapped Old Ma Greevy as well!' says Dev. 'And they're keeping her locked up somewhere. So she doesn't boil them in oil.'

'Or maybe she's just a nice old lady who likes dogs,' sighs Jasmine.

'Well, whatever she is, she's not here now,' I say, ducking down as a bunch of dogs come bounding towards the window, barking their heads off. They must have heard us talking. Poor things.

They look really hungry. We've got to get them out of here. Now.

I straighten up again and head for the nearest door. Locked. The front one is too.

'Time for back-up,' I announce, pulling out my mobile and dialling.

'Emergency services,' says the operator. 'Which service do you require?'

'The police,' I blurt. 'Wait, make that detectives. There are heaps of kidnapped victims here. Maybe send some ambulances as well.'

Jasmine's making whooshing movements in my face with her hands.

'Hang on a minute,' I say to the operator.

I put my hand over the mouthpiece, then bark 'What!?' at Jasmine.

'The fire brigade,' she says.

I stare at her.

'We might need their ladders,' she explains. 'To break in through the roof.'

'And the fire brigade,' I tell the operator. 'Actually, send everything you've got.'

I spend the next few minutes describing exactly where we are. Then we head back to our window, and wait for them all to turn up.

▲ ▲ ▲

Nine minutes tick past. Then ten. Nobody's arrived. Not even the detectives.

Then one of the dogs starts barking. Really loudly. *Yap! Yap! Yap!*

I peek through the window again. The leaping dog I saw before springs straight at me. Just as well there's glass between us. I'm not sure I could handle being kissed by a dog twice in one day.

'Hey! Check him out!' Dev says as the dog backs slowly away, his eyes never leaving my face. Then he runs to a door on the other side of the room, and stands right in front of it.

His front paw goes up and he's pointing—I'm not joking here—*pointing* at the door. It's like he's trying to tell me something. Awesome!

'Come on,' I tell the others. 'There's got to be a way in somewhere.'

'Try the window maybe?' says Dev.

The window! Why didn't I think of that? I give it a push and it slides straight up. We clamber through and race across to the door.

And guess what's on the other side? Old Ma

Greevy. Slumped on the floor, right next to her bed. OMG. I hope she's okay!

A-pocketa-pocketa-pocketa!

We run outside. Helicopters are circling the property. Then the Tactical Response Unit arrives, followed closely by the Bomb Disposal Squad, a fleet of ambulances and a fire engine.

We tell the ambos about Old Ma Greevy and pretty soon she's being whisked off to hospital. So that's all good. The head of the Bomb Squad tells us she's decided to cancel the lecture she was going to give us on Wasting Police Time. She reckons we probably saved Mrs Greevy's life. She even calls us heroes!

Then one of the detectives asks if we can stay with the dogs while they send out the Dog Control Unit. They're going to a shelter until Mrs Greevy's well enough to look after them again. So we stay.

And that's when I see it. A poster on the wall. A *circus* poster.

And the dog on the poster is the one that's in the room with us right now! He *is* a circus dog!

'Nutbush?' I call softly. And he runs straight to me, leaps up into my arms, and licks my ear.

That's when I get my second brilliant idea.

THE AMAZING NUTBUSH

DOES THE NUTBUSH!

I hope Mrs Greevy wakes up soon. I need to ask her something really important.

▲ ▲ ▲

The big day has finally arrived. Dunedoo State School's Best-trained Dog Competition. And this year, they've decided to hold it in the Dunedoo

Senior Citizen's Centre. Which is actually kind of perfect for me. Senior Citizens are about the only people on Earth who actually remember what the Nutbush is.

My Nanna Mo is all over it though. She even showed me some of the moves. It's this dance people used to do way back in the Dark Ages. You stand in lines and kick your legs out and jump around a bit. It's awesome.

Nutbush moved in to our place two days after we rescued Mrs Greevy. She said I could look after him till she's better. And if that works out well, she might even let me adopt him!

As soon as I put the Nutbush music on, he jumped down off the couch and started doing the steps. I didn't even have to train him!

The MC taps the microphone. 'Next up we have . . . Sam and his Amazing Wonderdog, Nutbush!'

The music starts up. Dev and Jasmine give me a big thumbs up from the side of the stage. And we're on! Nutbush is up on his hind legs, kicking and jumping like crazy. And I'm right there beside him.

And then something really incredible happens. All the Senior Citizens jump up out of their chairs and join in. Including the ones with dodgy hips. They're loving it!

I even spot Mrs Pumphrey in the back row, jiggling along to the music. And then I notice something else. Something I thought I'd never see. Flossy and Zippy are with her, on leashes! They're both up on their hind legs, shimmying along beside her.

It's a Nutbush Knockout!

We win the contest. Boof and Crusher's act was going really well, until Boof accidentally gave the wrong hand signal. Crusher peed on a Senior Citizen's wheelie walker, and they got disqualified.

Mrs Martini calls Nutbush and me back up onto the stage to accept our Golden Dog Biscuit trophy. Yes!

Jasmine and Dev give me a thumbs up from the side of the stage. And for one golden moment, I swear Nutbush does too.

CHARLIE AND THE STATIONS OF THE CROSS-COUNTRY

by

Alan Brough

I closed the book I had been reading.

RUNNING AWAY FROM THINGS

By Dr Clifford Von Odets Jnr

How to run away from terrifying things
that are absolutely, certainly going
to kill you

Property of
Charlie Ian Duncan
DO NOT STEAL

Running Away From Things includes tips on how to run away from all sorts of terrifying things that are absolutely, certainly going to kill you: angry snakes, very upset rhinos, angry snakes riding very upset rhinos, mentally unstable octopuses throwing angry snakes off the back of very upset rhinos, Komodo dragons with lawnmowers, and many, many more things that are, as I said before, really, very, super, absolutely, certainly going to kill you.

I stayed up all night finishing *Running Away From Things*.

I had to finish it.

I had to finish it because I needed all the help I could get.

In a few hours I was going to face the biggest challenge of my life.

I was going to run the school cross-country.

And I couldn't get out of it.

It was compulsory.

The word 'compulsory' is one of my least favourite words. My least-favourite other words include:

- Run Charlie! (Usually said by my best friend Hils when something painful is about to happen to me.)

- Eye-pus! (Usually said by my best friend Hils after something painful has happened to me.)
- Laugh-snot. (Usually coming out the nose of my best friend Hils after something painful has happened to me.)
- Frigate. (I once said it to my teacher Mrs Bigge-Crabbe and she thought I said a rude word and sent me to the principal. Frigate is not a rude word. I said it because Hils and I were having a competition to see who could name the most types of boats. Hils won.)

▲ ▲ ▲

I am no good at running.

So I do not do running.

Because I do not do running I don't know anything about running. (Apart from the fact that I don't do it.)

I *had* to run the cross-country. So I *had* to learn something about how to do running.

Running Away From Things is the only book I own that has the word 'running' in the title.

Luckily, *Running Away From Things* includes a number of tips about how to do running.

I decided to follow all the *Running Away From Things* tips.

I had to.

Or else the cross-country would kill me.

Other things that you are forced to do at school—apart from the cross-country—that can kill you:

- Anything that Hils says 'will be fun'.
- All sport.
- Anything that Hils says 'will be interesting'.
- Photocopying your bottom or any other part of your body. (In his book *Photocopiers Are Going To Kill You*, Dr Clifford Von Odets Jnr says that putting your bottom on a photocopier can give you Posterior Light Poisoning. This can be fatal.)
- Anything that Hils says 'will not kill you'.

▲ ▲ ▲

Our school doesn't have big grounds so we do our cross-country at a place called Wattle Park.

To get to Wattle Park we have to take a bus from the school.

As I was waiting to get on the bus, my best friend Hils was escorted to the front of the line by a teacher.

Hils was on crutches.

When I finally got on the bus I sat down next to Hils.

(The seat next to Hils was empty. The seat next to Hils is always empty.)

'Hils!' I said as I sat down. 'You've broken your leg!'

'Negative,' said Hils. (Hils says 'negative' instead of 'no' and 'affirmative' instead of 'yes' because that is what they say in the army. Hils really wants to join the army. She acts like she is already in the army.)

'You won't be able to run the cross-country,' I said.

'Negative,' said Hils.

'Brilliant,' I said. 'I wish I'd thought of that . . . wait a minute . . . when I said, "You've broken your leg", you said "negative". So, you haven't broken your leg?'

'Affirmative.'

'Then why are you on crutches? Why is your leg in plaster?'

'To make running the cross-country more challenging,' said Hils.

'But running the cross-country is already really, very, super challenging,' I said.

'Negative.'

'It's going to be impossible on crutches . . . with one leg in plaster,' I said.

'Negative.

'There is something wrong with you, Hils.'

'Affirmative,' said Hils. 'And there's something wrong with you too. You're wearing a dress.'

'It's a *skirt,*' I said. I know a lot more about ladies' clothes than Hils. Some people find this surprising. I don't. Hils doesn't either.

I was wearing a skirt because of *Running Away From Things*.

▲ ▲ ▲

RUNNING AWAY FROM THINGS
Tip One
When running, always wear clothes that blend in with your surroundings.

Wattle Park is a park.

To blend in with the park surroundings I was wearing a brown skirt (to blend in with the dirt and sandpits; to make sure it blended in with the sandpits I had stuck a brown plastic bulldozer to the skirt), a blue, sparkly, plastic top hat (to blend in with the sky), a green fluffy cardigan (to blend in with the grass), one grey sock (to blend in with the murky pond in the middle of the park) and one stripy, multi-coloured sock (to blend in with the playground next to the car park).

As I was getting off the bus I tripped on the hem of my skirt and fell out of the bus and onto the ground.

'Your skirt will not be easy to run in,' said Hils as she crutched off the bus.

'I will be fine,' I said.

'Did your skirt once belong to a tuna?' said Hils.

'No,' I said. 'It was my uncle's.'

'Then why do you smell of tuna?' said Hils.

'Two reasons,' I said. 'The first reason is because I have empty tuna tins sellotaped to the toes of my gumboots.'

▲ ▲ ▲

RUNNING AWAY FROM THINGS
Tip Two
When running, always wear strong running shoes. (Steel-capped running boots are best.)

'I don't have any steel-capped running boots,' I said to Hils.

'I do,' said Hils.

That did not surprise me.

'So,' I said. 'I got a pair of Dad's gumboots and sellotaped empty tuna tins to the toes instead.'

'That is not a strategically sound plan,' said Hils.

'That is not a strategically sound plan' is the army way of saying 'sellotaping empty tuna tins to a pair of your dad's gumboots is dumb.'

'The second reason I smell of tuna,' I said, 'is because I *am* a tuna.'

'Negative. You are not a tuna.'

'Please be supportive, Hils.'

'Negative.'

▲ ▲ ▲

RUNNING AWAY FROM THINGS
Tip Three
Think fast.

'My book told me that if I wanted to be a fast runner then I should think like things that are fast runners and that would make me a fast runner. I watched a program about sharks and the sharks were chasing some tuna. The tuna were fast,' I said.

'Tuna are fast', said Hils. 'They're just not fast *runners*.'

'Good point,' I said. 'I am a leopard.'

'Don't you mean a cheetah?' said Hils.

'Do I mean a cheetah?'

'Affirmative. Cheetahs are the fastest of all land animals.'

‘That’s very fast,’ I said.

‘Affirmative.’

‘I don’t think I need to be *that* fast. Are leopards still pretty fast?’

‘Affirmative.’

‘I could be a piglet. Piglets are fast.’

‘They’re not as fast as leopards,’ said Hils.

‘I am a piglet!’ I said.

‘I think you should stick with being a leopard,’ said Hils.

‘I could be a piglet being chased by a leopard,’ I said.

‘I don’t think you completely grasp the concept of thinking fast,’ said Hils.

‘I think you are right.’

Hils and I were almost at the cross-country starting line. Most of my class were already waiting to start. Some were jogging on the spot. Some were stretching. Townes MacFarlane had put his shorts on the wrong way and was trying to get them on the right way without taking them off and showing everyone his ‘Bananas in Pyjamas’ underpants. He was not succeeding.

I stopped.

I took off my backpack and took out a huge bottle of water.

▲ ▲ ▲

RUNNING AWAY FROM THINGS
Tip Four
Before you run, make sure you are thoroughly hydrated.

I lifted the huge bottle of water to my lips. A tsunami of water poured into my mouth. I started swallowing as fast and as much as I could.

I am okay at drinking water. I'm not amazing at it. I'm just normally good.

Being normally good at drinking water was not good enough for the amount of water that was now pouring down my throat.

I desperately tried to drink it all.

I choked.

I gasped.

I choked some more.

But I was still managing to drink a lot of the water.

I drank and drank and drank until I was completely full of water. Really, very, super uncomfortably full of water.

(This must be what it feels like to be an aquarium.)

I had done it.

I had made sure I was thoroughly hydrated.

▲ ▲ ▲

RUNNING AWAY FROM THINGS

Tip Five

When you start running, run as fast as you can for as long as you can for as far as you can.

'On your marks . . .' said Mr Stop-Sine.

My class got ready to start the cross-country. Everyone was jostling for position. I had never really jostled before. I did not like it. Hils was jostling using her crutches. (Actually, she wasn't really jostling at all. She was whacking and poking and prodding and tripping and squeezing Harriet Borges' head by using the crutches like giant chopsticks.) I did not think that was in the spirit of jostling.

'Get set . . .'

I was dressed to blend in with my surroundings, I was wearing steel-capped running boots, I was thinking like a piglet that was being chased by a leopard, and I was thoroughly hydrated.

'Go!'

I started running.

As fast as I could. As long as I could. As far as I could.

I was *running*.

It wasn't as awful as I thought it would be. It was actually okay.

I ran past Hils on her crutches.

'I'm running!'

'Affirmative,' said Hils.

Then I ran past Simon Bolivar.

Wait a minute. I ran *past* Hils. I ran *past* Simon Bolivar.

I RAN PAST TWO PEOPLE! I RAN PAST TWO PEOPLE WHO WERE MOVING!

'I AM A LEOPARD!' I shouted at Simon Bolivar as I ran past.

Simon Bolivar screamed. He screams when anything happens to him. Anything.

I was running as fast as I could and I was REALLY, VERY, SUPER FAST.

I ran past Harriet Borges.

'BITE MY TOE-CANS!' I shouted at her.

I ran past Krishna Malhotra.

'EAT SKIRT-DUST!'

I ran past Townes MacFarlane.

'PIGLET POWER!'

I ran past Junior Silesi.

'I'M A TUNA WITH LEGS!' I yelled.

I ran past my friend Rashid.

'I'M A CARDIGAN OF FIRE!'

I kept on running.

Then I realised that there was no one in front of me.

I turned and looked.

Everyone was behind me.

I was in the lead.

I was winning.

I WAS WINNING!

I started to run even faster.

I was *running*. I was a *runner*.

I started to run even, even faster.

I was *sprinting*. I was a *sprinter*.

I *was* faster than a piglet.

I was the fastest thing on earth.

Then it happened.

My legs started to wobble. Just a little bit. They still felt like my legs. Just a wobbly version of my legs.

Then they started to wobble a bit more than a bit. A lot of a bit. I was still running but now my legs didn't feel like *my* legs any more. They felt like they had a mind of their own. A mind of their own that was making them wobble a lot of a lot.

My knees wobbled in towards each other. Like they were having a talk. A talk about whether to recommend to the rest of my legs that they keep on wobbling or that they do something else.

I think my knees recommended the rest of my legs do something else because all of a sudden my legs stopped wobbling.

Then they stopped running.

Then they stopped moving at all.

Then they just stood there.

I had stopped running as fast as I could.

I had stopped running as long as I could.

I had stopped running as far as I could.

My friend Rashid ran past me.

Junior Silesi ran past me.

Townes MacFarlane ran past me.

Krishna Malhotra ran past me.

Harriet Borges ran past me.

Simon Bolivar ran past me. (He screamed.)

Then Hils crutched past me.

'Help!' I shouted to Hils. 'I'm not a piglet any more.'

▲ ▲ ▲

My legs were completely frozen.

I was going to be stuck here. Forever. Well, actually that wasn't exactly right. I was going to be stuck here until I died and I was pretty sure I was going to die soon. So, at least I wouldn't be stuck here forever. Soon I'd be in a coffin. But maybe I'd never be found and my body would be eaten by a piglet. Or a leopard. Or shared between a piglet and a leopard.

Yes, I was going to be eaten by a piglet and a leopard. For sure.

To make things worse, not only was I going to die and be eaten by a piglet and a leopard, but suddenly I was busting to go to the toilet.

▲ ▲ ▲

Then I had an idea.

It was probably the last idea I was going to have before dying and being eaten by a piglet and leopard.

'Legs,' I said to my legs. 'You have to move or else I am going to have to do a wee all over you.'

My legs didn't move.

'Legs, I promise, I solemnly swear that if you get me to a toilet I will never, ever do running again even though I was really, very, super good at it for a tiny, little while.'

My legs moved.

'I won't do dancing either.'

My legs moved some more. They moved so much some-more that I was walking.

'I'll always take the lift and never the stairs.'

My legs started to jog.

'Every morning I'll rub you with special leg cream.'

My legs started to run.

I ran past Hils.

I ran past Simon Bolivar. (He screamed.)

I ran past Harriet Borges.

I ran over the finishing line.

I ran into the toilet.

▲ ▲ ▲

'Charlie,' said Hils.

'Hils, you should not be in the boys' toilet,' I said.

'I'm not,' said Hils. 'You are in the girls' toilet.'

'Sorry about that,' I said.

'Apology accepted,' said Hils.

'Hils,' I said, 'I came third-to-last.'

'Affirmative.'

'I don't think I will ever do better than that.'

'Affirmative.'

'I am going to retire from running,' I said.

'Affirmative.'

ABOUT THE AUTHORS

Andy Griffiths

Andy Griffiths is one of Australia's most popular children's authors. From his bestselling, award-winning Treehouse series—now published in more than 30 countries—to the JUST! books (both illustrated by long-time friend and collaborator Terry Denton) and *The Day My Bum Went Psycho*, Andy's books have captivated and kept Australian kids laughing for more than 20 years. Andy's books have been *New York Times* bestsellers, adapted for stage and television and won over 70 Australian children's choice awards. Andy, a passionate advocate for literacy, is an ambassador for The Indigenous Literacy Foundation and The Pyjama Foundation.

The Three Stooges. *Adventure Time*. Pippi Longstocking. The Beastie Boys. The bewildered expression on my dog's face the time it slid down the slide in the playground. Stuff like that.

R. A. Spratt

R. A. Spratt is the author of the Nanny Piggins and Friday Barnes series of books. Before becoming an author, she worked as a television comedy writer. R. A. lives in Bowral with her husband, two daughters, three chickens, two goldfish and a desperately needy dog called Henry. She enjoys gardening and napping, but rarely gets the time to do either because her children are constantly asking her to make them snacks.

When someone hurts themselves.
It cracks me up every time.

John Marsden

John Marsden is the author of the bestselling The Tomorrow series and many award-winning titles. He lives in the Macdeon Ranges, just outside of Melbourne, where he is the principal of two schools, Candlebark and Alice Miller Schools—described by John as his proudest achievements. In 2014, John published his first novel for adults, *South of Darkness*. This book won the Fellowship of Australian Writers Christina Stead Award for Best Australian Novel of the Year.

Politicians, but not in a good way. Cats on YouTube. Knock-knock jokes (but only the funny ones). Puns, bloopers, Jane Austen, and *The Simpsons*.

Alex Ratt

Alex Ratt is the pen-name of award-winning author Frances Watts. Alex has written the stupendously smelly books *The Stinky Street Stories* and *2 Stinky* (illustrated by Jules Faber). Frances's books, which are far more fragrant, have won the Children's Book Council of Australia Book of the Year award and the Prime Minister's Award for Children's Fiction, and have been shortlisted for literary and children's choice awards around Australia.

I laugh in the face of danger, chortle in the face of diving pigs, guffaw in the face of indignant ducks, giggle in the face of tuna fish milkshakes and split my sides in the face of giant pickles.

Tristan Bancks

Tristan Bancks is a children's and teen author with a background in acting and filmmaking. His books include the My Life series, *Mac Slater Coolhunter* (Australia and US), *Two Wolves* and *The Fall*. *Two Wolves* was Honour Book in the 2015 Children's Book Council of Australia Book of the Year Awards and won YABBA and KOALA Children's Choice Awards. Tristan is excited by the future of storytelling and inspiring others to create. You can connect with Tristan, learn more about his books, play games and watch videos at www.tristanbancks.com

I LOVE stand-up comedy. I like humour that shocks and surprises me. I can't help but laugh when things go wrong! As a kid I was a HUGE fan of Roald Dahl, Paul Jennings and MAD Magazine. And, now, David Walliams's books make me laugh out loud.

Deborah Abela

Deb has always been short and a bit of a coward, which is why she writes books about spies, flooded cities and surviving Hitler's bombing raids. Her crankiness about climate change led to the novels *Grimsdon* and *New City*, and her own family's survival in World War Two inspired *Teresa: A New Australian*, about one very brave girl who migrates to Australia after her own country lies in ruins. Her latest books are *The Stupendously Spectacular Spelling Bee* and a picture book called *Wolfie, An Unlikely Hero*. Deb has won awards for her writing but mostly hopes to be as brave as her characters.

www.deborahabela.com

I like to laugh a lot but there are some things that always make me laugh. My partner (who thinks he's especially funny), riding my bike fast down hills, getting caught in storms during hikes, pigeons, busting uncool dance moves with friends, and goats in videos. Although, in real life, they can be a bit scary.

Tony Wilson

Tony Wilson is the author of many books, including *The Cow Tripped Over the Moon*, *Emo the Emu*, *Harry Highpants* and The Selwood Boys series. He is thinking of making a movie adaptation that mashes all of his books together, starring four footballing brothers wearing high pants who trip over the moon while riding an unhappy emu. This project is still in development. Tony's 2018 titles are *Hickory Dickory Dash* (Scholastic) and *Jed Kelly* (Lake Press). The thing Tony likes best about writing is telling people he's doing it while he's really having lunch.

www.tonywilson.com.au

The funniest thing I have ever seen is a YouTube video where a dog called Fenton chases deer. Also—bonsai plants (so weird), mobile phones in old movies (so big!), and kids accidentally crashing into each other in school musicals (so funny!). My son Harry makes me laugh all the time. He's eight, and when I asked him, 'What shall I write about for this book?' he casually replied, 'Sir Bum,' and kept on walking. This one's for you, Harry!

Meredith Costain

Meredith Costain has been writing stories and poems since she was six but would like to stop soon as her arm is getting tired. She lives in a big, old house with a menagerie of pets, who frequently wrangle their way into her stories. Her books include the quirky illustrated series The Ella Diaries, *Disaster Chef*, CBCA Honour Book *Doodledum Dancing*, and novelisations of the TV show *Dance Academy*. She loves sleeping, reading, playing blues piano, and searching for the perfect chocolate bar.

www.meredithcostain.com

When my pets do funny and unexpected things, like the day my cat Harriet ambushed my dog Jack, lying in wait behind a bush and jumping out at him as he happily trotted past. Jack jumped a mile!

And also stories that have words with double meanings in them, like the one about the two vomits. Have you heard it?

Two vomits were walking down the street. The first vomit started crying.

'What's wrong?' asked the second vomit.

The first vomit sniffled sadly. 'I was brought up around here.'

Alan Brough

Alan Brough was born in New Zealand and is quite a bit older than he'd like to be. Alan has always loved books and, from an early age, wanted to be a writer. Then he and his Dad went to see *Star Wars* and Alan decided that, actually, he really, really, really, really, really, really, really wanted to be an actor.

After having been an actor for a while Alan realised there wasn't that much work for a 6-foot 4-inch guy with a slightly lopsided face and thick curly hair so he tried his hand at directing, broadcasting, composing, dancing (true!), singing and, in an unexpected turn of events, being a professional music nerd.

Recently, he got around to being a writer.

One day he hopes to have a bio that includes phrases like 'bestselling', 'award-winning' and 'so successful that he recently bought a solid-gold toilet'. Until then, he's just happy to look at his copies of *Charlie and the War Against the Grannies* and *Charlie and the Karaoke Cockroaches* and think, 'Cool! I wrote a book. And then another book!'

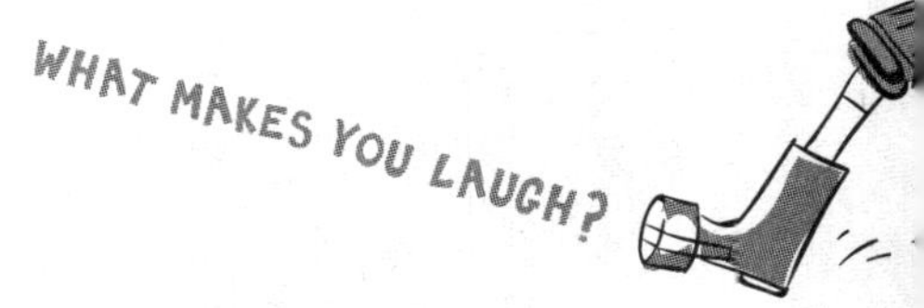

I make *me* laugh.

Not in a 'I am sooooo funny' sort of way. More in a 'I am suuuuch an idiot' sort of way.

A few weeks ago I was going to make a cup of tea and I was looking for my mug. My favourite mug. The only mug I like drinking out of.

But I couldn't find it. I looked around the kitchen. It wasn't there.

I looked on my desk. It wasn't there. I looked next to the chair where I sit and read. It wasn't there.

Where was it?

I looked all over the house. I even checked behind the toilet.

I just couldn't find my mug.

I decided that someone must have broken into my house to steal my mug. That was the only logical explanation. I thought about calling the police. I thought about getting a guard dog. I thought about fitting GPS trackers to all the other mugs in the house.

Later that night I opened the microwave and there was my mug.

I quickly cancelled my online order for 15 GPS trackers. Then I started laughing. At myself.

I am suuuuch an idiot.

ABOUT THE ILLUSTRATOR

Andrea Innocent

Andrea Innocent began professionally illustrating after returning from living in Japan in 2006. Her personal illustrations tell stories of Japanese ghosts, folktales and depict quirky newspaper articles. Her commercial work covers many areas from editorial illustration to animation. Clients include Microsoft, The Melbourne Recital Centre, Malvern Star, *Rolling Stone Magazine*, *The Australian* and *The Age*. She is also a member of The Jacky Winter Group in Melbourne.

Andrea has also given talks and workshops on all sorts of topics related to illustration and design, such as professional practice, drawing, marketing and character design. She also teaches part-time.

She is currently working from her home studio in the hills with her partner, her son, elderly cat and her Welsh Cardigan Corgi 'Pickles McGerkin'.

www.andreainnocent.com

What makes me laugh are sports mascots, particularly Japanese baseball characters. It's something about the enormous head, usually being held up by tiny, comical looking arms and the completely uncoordinated way they run around and into things. That's what makes me laugh, that and making food into a face :-).

THE
END